# *The*
# Light Man
## *and the*
# Hidden Face

El Hadji Seydou Mbaye

Fulton Books
Meadville, PA

Published by Fulton Books 2024

ISBN 979-8-89221-701-9 (paperback)
ISBN 979-8-89221-702-6 (digital)

Printed in the United States of America

Tribute to anyone who has sacrificed part of his life, with visible or hidden works, for the good of humanity.

*Wherever you turn, the face of God is there.*
—(Quran, S2: V115

*And we have not sent you, (O Muhammad),*
*except as a mercy to the worlds.*
—Quran, S21: V107

# Contents

# The Face of the Secret

In front of the destructive madness of the human being—his caprices, his fantasies, his ignorance—a decree came from above. In addition to the prophets who had the mission to preach the divine message, a group of individuals, men of enlightenment, was dispatched to accompany the masses.

Order of mission: to act in the face of excess, to preserve as best as possible what the prophets had elaborated.

Individuals were chosen for each generation with different missions.

Already, in the afterlife, the archangel had briefly explained to them their potential, that of man of light. They were born on earth in different continents. They had traveled the world to find their identities. They had lived ridiculous lives, but they had managed to overcome.

Thus, the three spheres spirits—27, 248, and 32816030716040716—respectively under the human names of Inse, Al-Amine, and Arbiz, had rediscovered their missions. Inse, passionate about knowledge, knew himself from now on. After arriving at the point of no desire, he had finally seen what was behind the curtain. As a result, he was reborn with a new vision of the world. Al-amine, in search of beauty around the world, after so much energy, finally found the scepter of the deity from which emanated all the beauty of the earth, the symbol of this ultimate beauty. He had returned to his country, burying the secret in the depths of his being. As for the third, Arbiz, the Qutb zamane, or the pole of time, which united all the human virtues in him, could have to teach his

1

knowledge to receptive people. His transmitted knowledge finally allowed him to rest.

Finally, they understood what was hiding between the three sentences: *A secret is a secret. A secret is a secret! A secret is a secret?*

*****

Time had passed, and the world had changed.

New societal ideologies came from everywhere. Endless conflicts pitted several nations around the world. A difference of opinion, ethnic group, religion, race, or culture was enough to trigger a war. No country was safe from this lapse. Each claimed to be the most perfect because of its cunning resources and methods.

International organizations were created, but none of them could find balance despite endless congresses.

The war was latent, and the weapons had become mass destruction.

# Onirocriticism and the Dream

With a start, he sat down on the bed. It looks like a nightmare. A long moment passed without him doing anything. A moment later, he pulled the drawer out of the dresser and pulled out an old book. He spent the rest of the night flipping through the book.

The next day, at noon, he went to a great marir-mushir to clarify his iterative dreams.

The scholar welcomed him and listened attentively. For him, it was an imminent disaster that was going to affect the whole earth, destroying almost everything in its path; but at the end of the dream, the same character who was named the first great guardian asked him to find the key of the heavenly chest to prevent the sinister.

It was the first time he had heard of a heavenly chest and a great guardian, but the scholar confirmed their existence, even though they were almost forgotten by most of their fellow creatures. He also told him that it was not a dream because the dream of the first great guardian is a reality, and to appease his soul, it was necessary to execute the injunction.

To better guide himself, he followed the advice of the great scholar who announced to him, "Every year, there is a special night that is worth over a thousand months and during which angels descend on earth, bringing divine mercy. It must be located in the last ten days of the month of fasting. Using your ectoplasmic echo-location will allow you to locate in space these mystic unsuspected characters."

His ordeal was growing because he did not know how to use his being to see the invisible. The pale veil that covered his eyes prevented him from seeing beyond his common world, yet he was a beloved of God, but his station was limited to subtle worlds, and not essences.

Sexagenarian, his body showed the stigmata of life by the wrinkles but also by the loss of any rigor of the youth.

The gloomy gaze, in the position of reflection and the wandering spirit, he reveled in his first memories of mission. The dreams that always haunted him did not change the injunctions. *He had to find the guardian of the heavenly chest.* Such a mission proved perilous as the latter was no longer known by evil spirits or men. His treasure had already sparked every imaginable conflict. Entire lines of species had already been decimated. Few new survivors of different worlds suspected its existence. For some, it was only fables or myths of the ancients and that times were over; for others, it still existed but veiled by the mystery of the sky.

Who was right? Mystery!

Even though he was not discouraged, his discomfort with his insomnia and his risk of depression forced him to go in search of this mystery in order to solve the greatest threat of the times to com: a third planetary war that would take everything in its path. The weapons had become sophisticated, and their destructive abilities were massive. Such a war was inevitable unless the great guardian could use his powers and his key to avert this unfortunate fate.

He was the only one to have such power, but where to look for it? And who was he?

Having only the eclocalization tool *"ectoplasmic,"* which he did not know the operation, his quietude seemed to leave him completely. Nevertheless, he kept the faith. His dreams were so recurring that he wondered if they were real.

Yet the scholar he had consulted had told him, *"The mysteries of the worlds can only be accessible to scholars. We can dream, imagine, but there is only the real."*

It was, for him, a simple sentence but difficult to decipher. He said to himself in his head, and according to common educational principles, there was reality, dreams, and the imaginary or utopia. These two versions seemed to contradict each other, but he knew that the scholar knew well what he was saying because he insisted on fixing it in his eyes as if he wanted to say to him, "*Go to the quest for the knowledge of secrets supreme.*"

According to his dreams, he was the only person on earth able to go to this mystical treasure. Perhaps his will would allow him to succeed.

The treasure could move with anyone, but its concealment transcended the tools of ordinary mortals. Unsuspected he was with his very young age, isolated in the depths of the desert, even the evil creatures—with all their arsenal and fluidity through different worlds—failed to trace its hidden halo. Angels in tight rows protected his angelic vault in the darkness.

Weary of having searched all the earth and to have watched all the human beings, the hordes of demons decided to start a total war in order to annihilate everything and to finish, once and for all, this mystery.

Whispers began to blow on knots. Some leaders of major belligerent countries began to prepare for the worst. Coded messages circulated on both sides of the borders. The tensions became more and more electric. No peaceful solution was envisaged by the various antagonists because the damage was already immense. It was a spying of military maneuvers that went wrong.

Historically speaking, these two great powers were allies to fight a common enemy who wanted to impose his racial supremacy. After their victory, they shared the land. Each of them wanted to seize more territories. Thus, the whole globe was split into two large blocks.

"*Either you are with us, or you are against us.*" This was the adage they uttered.

Most of the weak countries were in line, each with hope of survival. Weapons of massive destruction were blown into the hearts of these belligerents. So it had become a frantic race. Without valid reasons, everyone could destroy the whole Earth more than a thousand times. All kinds of weapons concealment strategies were developed. Planes, ships, submarines, battle tanks, secret military bases, and even some satellites possessed their mysteries. No one was safe from this noise, even those who claimed to be non-allies.

One day, while one of the blocks was doing its military maneuver, the other was spying on it with its nuclear submarines. It must be remembered that here, each submarine possessed the arsenal that could shave an entire block when there were more than a hundred in the ocean. The training area was huge, but the participants managed to locate themselves thanks to their secret technologies. Each group tried to hide in the depths in order to surprise the other. Surface ships also participated in the maneuvers. Shots were exchanged between ships as in a real war, but the bullets were fake.

Unsuspected and hidden between the meshes, emerging from the great depths, submarines of the other block spied the strategies of war that their adversary undertook. Their approaches were undetectable, thanks to the technological ability of their submarines to reach unsuspected depths.

The maneuvers went as planned, and the end was announced. Suddenly, a ship detected foreign signals. The alert was given. The warships identified one by one, but a few remained silent. The count of beacons received exceeded the starting number. So the intruders were detected, and it was the real war.

What was initially simulations became an exchange of real torpedoes. Thus, ships were sunk on both sides. The less numerous intruders finally took off. The staffs of both blocks were briefed, and the presidents were brought to the secret bases built for these types of nuclear-threat conflicts.

The fugitives—with the smallness of their submarines, their high speeds, and their abilities to reach depths—disappeared into the abyss. The global alert was red. The nuclear suitcases were in the process of being used for the first time.

Global organizations, trying to calm the tension, were pushed aside. Negotiations between deaf-mutes and the blind were undertaken without any hope. It was in these circumstances that he wished to solicit the guardian of the safe.

After several attempts to search the tracks of the great guardian who had ended in failures, he was finally discouraged and resigned himself. Despite the repetitive dreams, he no longer listened to his heart. His enthusiasm dissipated, and his life became darker and darker as he was haunted by his own destiny that he did not want to accept.

*****

Months had passed since he met with onirotherapy.

One day, in the face of the insupportable heaviness of his head, he finally gave way to abandonment and went to the national library of the country to consult the books dealing with the subject of the great guardian and the celestial chest.

After several months of consultations, his astonishment was great. Despite the eight hours a day devoted to the subject, there was no guidance going to the hidden side. He was at the limit of his confidence and doubt began to settle in his head. To the point of removing all credibility from the scholar he had consulted, and in whom he had always trusted, the anecdote which the latter had told him, in order to give him hope and faith, came back to him.

He remembered the scholar's encouragement on the path of the hidden face.

*"It is not the way that is difficult, but rather it is the difficult that is the way,"* the scholar had told him.

The latter had watched him for a moment before continuing.

*"If one does not have deep faith, one will never go far because what is veiled by the mystery of the celestial vault transcends the eyes of the common man. You will need faith. It is the only mount to overcome the obstacles that dot the path."*

At the end of the scholar's recommendation, he was quick to shake his head as an affirmation before speaking again. *"I see. Now, what should I do?"*

*"Being aware of one's ignorance is the first step toward knowledge."* A moment of silence then he continued, *"Go first to the knowledge of the guidance, and your path will be more easily enlightened because the knowledge is the primordial lantern to guide itself."*

*"Do I have a way?"* asked the Sufi.

*"As long as your ego exists, all you will see is relative."*

7

He held his shoulder, followed by a brief moment of silence where he stared into his eyes before continuing. *"Know that the one who has fully realized the station of absolute servitude is exposed to the test."* He opened his eyes wide as a sign of astonishment. *"It will be necessary to know how to listen to the silence to be able to hear the rustling of the invisible. It can help you,"* added the scholar.

A gleam of misunderstanding appeared on his face. In this respect, the scholar encouraged him. *"Be brave. It is a virtue of great men."*

So the scholar gave him some instructions and prayed for him before letting him go. He left this journey of dreams and came back to his reality by sketching a big smile as if he had found his way. His discomfort was transformed into a hope that could be read in the features of his face.

# The Sign of Guidance

The first scholar he met described him as unfit for the task because the access levels he needed would be much higher than his. He inquired of the spiritual masters of his region, but none of them could satisfy him. Similarly, in his country and even in neighboring countries, but it was always the same answer:

*"What is veiled by the mysteries of the divine is not accessible to everyone,"* the scholar had told him.

Contrary to what he thought, his discomfort and confusion were growing.

*"There is no soul that perceives the sound of its sails without being annihilated,"* added the scholar.

He knew of no master who could deliver him from his extraordinary secrets that would require practically a lifetime, for most people, before he could access them, and those who know it were unknown to him.

One evening, in a state of meditation, an idea crossed him. It was to go to the mausoleum of the greatest scholar in their history and to formulate prayers of good guidance and vows.

The next day, he took a bush taxi and headed for the city of this great scholar who died two centuries ago. People regarded him as one of the great guardians and even as an exception in their hierarchy because he was called the supreme recourse of his time.

The taxi crossed the country and went to the neighboring country. When he arrived at his destination, he was exhausted because of his sitting position for two days. His trip showed his willingness to fight with his heavy burden.

In the mausoleum, in front of the saint's tomb, he took a seat in front of a pillar, on which he placed his body, showing the stigmata of the excursion. Prayer on prayers, incantations after incantations, he seemed to forget all his fatigue and only focused on the reasons for his displacement. A moment of silence, then he didzed, his rosary escaped him.

With a quick movement, he woke up and saw the rush of his pearls. He did not know how many incantations he had made and how much he had left. Thus, his conscience awoke. He now knows that everything had to be resumed in order to accede to the realization of the vows as do the followers of this erudition.

On three occasions, his experience remained the same. Fatigue had the upper hand over his desires. At the third sleep, a dream came to him. He saw an old man, dressed all in white, apparently the master of the house, patted his shoulder and woke him in the dream before speaking to him.

*"Whoever can give you guidance is in the orbit of the astroid. Its wake splits the darkness between dusk and dawn."*

*"Hum!"*

*"If you do not put effort on your signs, they will hide your light."*

Before disappearing, the old man finished his remarks. *"Listen to your heart because it is not a matter of being on a path, but rather of having the utility of a path, and there, only the heart can contain the utility.*

*****

Another waking alarm, which alerted the few present, he turned his head on all sides to stare at people. He was certain of the absence of his interlocutor in the dream. Thus, he packed his few belongings and left the scene.

He seemed to find his answers. The words were clear in his head, even if the old man spoke in parables. The overlapping of the words of the first scholar on the night of destiny and the information of his dream would allow him to find his initiatory master. However, the fasting month was not far away.

During the last ten days of the month of fasting, he was awake all night as he froze toward the starry sky. The galactic constellations seemed to be infinite. His contemplation carried him to galaxies for millions of years of light. This immensity turned out to be gleaming; this world had no end.

On the twenty-seventh day, an event occurred which changed the course of his destiny. As he scanned the clear sky, a shooting star crossed toward the west before splitting into four small pieces. This phenomenon was extremely rare. Providence appeared to him full of favors. He carefully observed the directions of the four smithereens and saw, in an unusual view, four light beams splitting the darkness toward specific points of the earth; it looks like four cardinal points. These efforts had paid off. These four points corresponded to the presence of these mystical scholars whom he had to meet in order to elucidate his mystery.

Seen from the sky, these points seemed close, but in reality, it was continental. He knew from now on that in his continent and in certain geographical zones, there were scientists able to teach him the use of his ectoplasmic echolocation, with supra-luminous dimension. This subtle knowledge, however, was only the stammering of his journeys because finding an individual incognito in a geographical area grouping several countries would prove perilous or impossible, but his faith to be assisted by providence became obvious. He heard about a great scholar in the neighboring country. He went there without waiting, but the latter told him that he was not one of those he was looking for, but that he could refine his guidance with a certain initiatory methodology.

In front of these remarks of luminous supplement, he could only accept.

"In your heart, erase all that is desire. Eliminate all that is passion. Do what you have to do. Calm down. Soothe yourself. Accept things to come without feelings. Contemplate them, and you will see," the master taught him.

*****

Months had passed, and his understanding of spiritual essences was increasing. He spent his days between loneliness, hunger, vigil, and silence. He ate only once a day and could stay days without speaking. Abstinence from speech could be done by isolating oneself, but according to one's master, one had to silence one's heart, and this would require great capacities of self-control.

He did not skimp on the sacrifices. So he climbed some stations and came to see each other. His soul was echoing, and his heart was its receptacle, like a modern radar system. He was able to switch from normal view to infrared, thermal view, and ultraviolet. He had the remaining supra-luminous visions, and such things could only be taught by his four points he had seen in the sky. However, he stayed a few months with this master to refine his contemplation of the hidden face of reality.

His master released him and wished him to meet those he was looking for. He took the path of great quests again with a valuable tool, that of echolocation.

# The Trip

O ne evening, he was inspired to continue on his way to new lands
to get closer to his goal. He took a bush taxi that he shared
with seven other passengers and the driver to another country. He
sat down on the front seat, next to the driver, whom he shared with
another traveler. It was very common to overload vehicles in this
region of the universe. Instead of five people, the car contained nine,
without counting the excess luggage. The car rolled all afternoon,
crossing a grassy savannah. The unpaved road was winding. The
orange solar disk gradually declined and disappeared on the horizon.
Without lampposts and with the absence of a moon, the environment sank into total darkness. The car was old, the electric system
did not work, and also the lights.

A moment later, in front of the total invisibility, the driver got
off the vehicle and mounted a battery torch on the front hood to get
a dozen meters of nitescence. The risk of hitting an obstacle was enormous, but in this geographical area, safety standards did not exist.

During the whole trip, they had met only two other vehicles
that were going in the opposite direction. However, the Sufi sank his
rosary with a certain misguidance of the spirit. So his mind was nav-
igating. Sometimes it was subtle things; sometimes it was out of the
ordinary. Suddenly, he had a vision. A man on a bicycle was driving
on the road. He turned his head slightly toward the driver and saw
that the driver was not too careful on the road. Since he had hardly
met anybody for several hours, he had relaxed despite a lesser view.

So the Sufi warned him, "There is a bicycle on the road."

Astonished, the driver threw himself forward, scanned the path,
but could not see anything. He turned slightly to the Sufi as stupid-

ity, but he did not answer this accusing look. Without decelerating and with less attention, the driver was acting as if nothing had happened. On the contrary, you could hear the engine boosting power. Suddenly, he narrowly avoided the driver of the bicycle who threw himself into the undergrowth. A look was exchanged between the driver and the Sufi.

In his head, questions flocked. *How could he see the bicycle that was more than two kilometers away and in the dark?* He kept twirling toward the Sufi after each question in order to find an answer in his imagination, but he remained dubious to his assaults. No other word was exchanged. The other passengers who were already sleeping on their seats had awoken by the bewilderment at the risk of accident.

An hour later, in a lost place, a truck was standing in the middle of the road. The driver was momentarily captivated, wondering about what had happened, while forgetting to concentrate on the road. Suddenly, the vehicle engine stopped running. The driver relaunched, but it creaked and went out. After several attempts, it was always the same result. He raised his head slightly and saw a truck in front of them without taillights. He knew at that moment that a few yards away was certain death. He exhaled to release his stupor. Everyone remained silent. Thus, he restarted the vehicle without result. He understood the origin of the sudden stop and the vehicle's failure. He turned his head toward the Sufi, without saying a word, and restarted the car. Thus done, he carefully skirted the lorry and left his mind open to the Sufi.

\*\*\*\*\*

In the middle of the night, he made a stop and allowed the passengers to drink. The rest was finally prolonged until dawn before resuming the road in the light of the rising sun.

\*\*\*\*\*

At the zenith, they finally entered a city. The Sufi went down, took his bag, and asked for the direction of the marketplace. He

said to himself that with the gathering of people coming from different zones, he could probably meet an august who could direct him
toward the receptacle of the city.

Throughout the rest of the afternoon, despite his echolocation,
he could not see anyone. He camped behind a merchant's table and
spent the night there.

A week passed without him seeing a single individual whom he
could suspect of mystical knowledge. One weekend, as the market square
was emptying of its occupants, he saw a handler dragging a wagon from
a distance. He changed his vision and switched from normal to infrared
to thermal and finally to ultraviolet as his master had taught him. This
brief diagnosis allowed him to detect a halo of light around the head of
the individual who was approaching. He intercepted and spoke to him.
After the greetings, he asked him where to find the receptacle of the city.
This question seemed to come from nowhere, and the passerby felt like
he was sounding because it was not common to be mistaken for a scientist with his way of life. He stammered by not letting out any words,
and then looked at the Sufi surprisingly. It was, thus, that he perceived
that they were similar. He ended up sending him the question, "What
was it about?" asked the passerby.

"About a quest for guidance in the area. I come from the neighboring country, and I do not know anything about it here." *His assistance will be valuable to me and would save me time.*

The passerby shook his head and seemed to understand it. "I
do not know who it is, but very often, once a year, in the night, I saw
a beam of light rising toward the sky. It must be located around the
public park."

With this exchange, they parted in a jovial air. For several days,
he frequented the park without distinction of hours.

One day, as he approached, he saw two individuals on the
same public bench in the park. His mind was attracted to something
bizarre. He changed his vision and zoomed in on the two individuals
and realized that one was bringing out a very dark ether of Gehenna
to transfer it to the other. In normal view, this phenomenon would
be unnoticed; but with his erudition, he could see it. While one went
out his evil ether, the other was illuminated more and was surrounded

by a luminous halo. The one with the ether read a newspaper while the other was immersed in a book. Everyone seemed to be busy with something else, but the spiritual battle was intense. The ether developed above the illuminated to form a dense black mass. Suddenly, he tried to penetrate the illuminated.

A kind of spark occurred, and the dark man threw down his newspaper with cries of agony. He was horrified and went into a demonic trance. All attention was attracted by his cries. Nobody knew what had taken him, but the Sufi had watched the whole scene and understood that the one he was looking for in the park was indeed illuminated.

The Sufi approached the sullen and held his hand. He instantly found his mind with a look of terror. He spoke to him. "Why do you want to transfer your pain?"

A shameful air overwhelmed him. He lowered his head and, in a low voice, answered the question without getting up from the ground, "Because I was possessed by demons during my nocturnal walks, and I do not know how to get rid of them. The only way I can temporarily calm my suffering is to contaminate others."

"Everyone is not the same. The image is only second nature."

"Now I know."

"Go get up and ask for forgiveness before her mind haunts you forever."

He stood up with an exhausted air and squatted again before the illuminated man who stopped him and freed him from his worries. He was forgiven and was advised to go on a healer's quest to get rid of his demons.

After the departure of the possessed, the Sufi took his place and presented himself to the illuminated, thus, began a long discussion. He told him about his journey and his misfortune, which had led him to the brink of *disgrace* despite the consultation of an oneiromancer scholar. He asked her for guidance. In this respect, the illuminated seemed to be very interested in what the newcomer was saying. For years, he was hardly disturbed in his isolation; he was unearthed by an individual from far away to intercede on a dangerous mission that was to be his. Thus, began a long series of questions and answers.

"How did you find me?" asked the illuminated.

"I followed the wake of the astroid."

"This is not enough because astroids cross the starry sky every night."

"This is another because it splits the darkness between dusk and dawn."

The enlightened man, hearing him speak in parables, allowed a smile to appear as if he had understood the very essence of his words.

"I see that you have been well-guided."

"He had taught me to pay attention to the slightest signs," said the Sufi.

"This is the only sign that could locate us, and it only happens once a year."

A moment of silence, then he continued, "This is the sign of grace."

"And since when do you live like this?" asked the Sufi.

"Since the beginning of my mission."

"Like this! You do not risk being assaulted?"

"You are the first person to see me as I am."

"Since when?"

"For a very long time. I can say always."

The Sufi did not add anything to it and remained meditative, while the illuminated man plunged back into his book. The minutes passed, then the illuminated closed the book and turned to the Sufi with a new question. "And why me?"

"I am looking for the guardian of the chest to use the key to divert this unfortunate destiny."

"Hum," said the illuminated without saying a word.

A moment later, in the face of indifference, the Sufi resumed, "I have been so searching, to the point of being tired."

A moment of silence, then he resumed the explanation with passion as if he was waiting for this moment to share his knowledge with someone motivated and who could hear it.

"I am not the guardian, but I will tell you the anecdote of the wishes of an octogenarian to revive your faith," said the illuminated.

# Wishes Granted

An old man of eighty was in a prayer position. Hair all white, wrinkled face, blurred vision, shaking gestures—he was on the edge of "disgrace" after a lifetime of faith. Sadness was on his face. The eyes revealed tears that could not flow. His high breathing was accelerated.

Ideas went through his head. He summed up his whole life, but no longer seemed satisfied. He focused on the four most popular targets but found he had not reached any of them. Throughout his life, he could not have a harem of beautiful women. He was not wealthy despite hard work for fifty years. He was not famous, otherwise no one knew him outside his workplace and neighborhood. He was not a scholar stuffed with diplomas. He had only one child, although he kept imploring the heavens to have seven.

Here he was, sitting to abdicate what he had sacrificed since taking responsibility. He was someone who had never missed a prayer. He gave alms to the needy. He forgave. He was always looking for the right way to follow, and he was following her. To see him practice such a life, he was considered pious. He never complained of what he could not have. He kept on hoping that his prayers would be answered. There, doubt settled in his head. He had always thought that *God's stores* were inexhaustible and were waiting to be used.

His faith had never faded until now. He thought he had been deceived by a whole religious system. He began to regret having deprived himself of certain vices without tangible results. He knew he could no longer go back to live a fulfilling youth. At his age, no woman would want him; he was old. He no longer had the strength to work to raise money. Wrinkles decorated him and baldness covered his head. He had no idea who could make him famous. No longer able to have a woman who could give him offspring with his eighty years, he no longer had the hope of having another child. He was conscious of having reproached himself for losing momentarily reason. With his Alzheimer's signs, he could no longer claim to study. His sacrifices seemed to him vain. He stammered words that could not get out of his mouth. The hesitation between his faith and doubt settled. After all, he did not know what was true or not.

Hands imploring heaven, he finally uttered his last prayer before deciding for his truth, "Lord, if you really exist, let me not doubt. Strengthen my faith and show me a sign so that I do not regret my sacrifices and prayers of the past. Lord, I have always believed, and I have always prayed. I tried to sow good wherever I was. I do not know what is true and what is not. Let me see, finally. You know better than anyone. Doubt begins to assail me."

In a sad voice, he finished his prayer, "I feel weakened."

As he said his prayers, a tear fell on his cheek. His growing despair could be seen on his flashing eyes. However, he did not want to be wrong. Suddenly, a winged humanoid, with a radiant face— half-man, half-woman—dressed simply, his head slightly inclined on the right shoulder, appeared to him. He slowly raised his head and saw it levitating. From a reflex, he tried to escape, but he was unable because he was paralyzed by a force he did not know.

It was the first time he had seen a man with wings, levitating. His intention was calmed by a small hand gesture from the stranger who reassured him not to be afraid before speaking. "I am the angel of vows, a kind of Santa Claus of big dimensions."

Mouth open, the old man could not believe his eyes. He wondered if he was dreaming. Thus, he frowned with both hands, but nothing had changed the scene. He tried to turn away, but the presence of this being seemed to occupy all directions. Immediately, with a peaceful voice, the angel answered his questioning. "You are not dreaming. It is true. You see me."

Without paying attention to the angel, he continued to check his condition. He bit his arm and saw that it was painful.

The angel finally landed on the earth and came to touch his hand. At that moment, he knew now that he was real. Thus, the angel continued, "Seeing you in disarray after so many years of effort, God summoned me to take stock of your prayers. He sent me to clarify your account. Your book of life shows that you are one of the beloved ones of God because all your prayers have been answered."

He was only waiting for that moment to jump with exclamation. "Me! My prayers accepted! No! No! All but that. I am old, but I still keep my head on my shoulders. I'm not fooled. I have not seen anything of it despite years of tireless work."

In an accusing tone, he attacked the angel. "I have always prayed. I always did what I had to do, but you forgot me. I was not discouraged to continue praying." He raised his voice and bitterness was in his voice. "In spite of everything, not only did you forget me, but you deprived me of the four great common goals."

The angel who could not be affected morally let him empty his bag before starting again. "The goal of my mission is to clarify your account."

He calmed down and stayed tuned.

"Indeed, you expected that one would grant your wishes according to a process that you had chosen. You wanted to be famous. God has granted you this prayer as compensation for your health. There were two choices: to be famous but sickly, depressed, and to be known only to those close to you, but in good health. God made you the best of choices because being famous, you will suffer throughout your life from drugs, failed suicide attempts, depression, lack of intimacy with the press, disappointment, and ubiquitous betrayals for fear of remaining so throughout your life. And despite everything, you will remain HIV-positive, hypertensive, and diabetic. Your health will not be able to support your celebrity, and since you are part of the beloved ones, God has realized the best of the choices."

"I had also asked to have children. I only have one!"

"Of course. For that too, God has accepted your prayers."

Without letting him finish, he cut him off with astonishment. "No! This is not accepted! I wanted at least seven. I know I will not be able to have any more."

Resembling someone who speaks to an unconscious child, the angel spoke again calmly, reiterating his message. "These prayers have been accepted. You were going to have seven children that you would cherish a lot, but they could not all survive. You would see them die horribly one by one. After their loss, you could not bear this grief. You would end up blaspheming, and that would bring you to hell. And since you are one of the beloved ones, God has made for you the best choice, to have only one child that you will not see die."

Throughout the angel's explanation, he saw himself in a big screen, experiencing all the processes. He did not doubt the purpose of each process that was displayed on the screen. A bitter feeling caught in his throat. With a voice convinced by the angel's explanations, he searched for something he had asked for in his memory that he had not been able to obtain.

With a spontaneous gesture, he spoke to the angel, "There is also the need for money. It was also part of my prayers."

"Like the two previous ones, these prayers were accepted."

"How come I am not rich, yet I worked fifty years? Without my retirement pension, I will not be able to survive."

"You are rich. It's because you do not see it from a certain angle. You have always supported your needs. Still, you manage to survive with what you earn. There were two choices: to be wealthy but not to enjoy life and spend all your time controlling your fortune, and the other choice is to support yourself and to be free to live and to go wherever you want and to somehow enjoy life. God has made for you the best choice since you are one of the beloved ones."

He looked for something else to add, but after each thought, his reason showed him that God's choice was more relevant than his own.

"To make it easier for you, it's the same for all the other prayers you had made. God answered them, and he made you the right choice. If you do not see what you're waiting for, it's because behind every choice you made, and you thought you were the right one, was a futility that, to your knowledge, is not worth it. God sent me so that you do not weaken. Your path is not vain."

He was now aware more than ever of the favors he had been able to benefit without realizing it. If he had been granted his vows as he conceived them, he would be among the losers. He turned to the angel with a big satisfying smile, mixed with a feeling of shame, for doubting. His heart kept begging his lord to forgive him for his ignorance.

*****

After the narration of the anecdote, the Sufi seemed to have answers to questions he had not asked yet. He shook his head in understanding. However, the illuminated man continued.

"You will need another star to continue your path," said the illuminated.

"Where to find it?"

"I cannot tell you more. Do what you did for me. I will rather advise you to further refine your knowledge."

The Sufi tried to ask another question that did not seem out of his mind. And it was to the enlightened to insist.

"Knowledge is the primordial lantern to strive toward its goal."

The Sufi raised his head before the illuminated man continued his explanation by staring into his eyes.

"He is the light of beings in the course of human formation."

He knew that he had a long way to go before he came to the top.

Time passed without words being exchanged. However, the illuminated man plunged back into his universe. His book seemed to captivate him. The Sufi, as for him, navigated in his past. Thus, he remembered the words of the great master who said to him, *"If you do not put effort on your signs, they will hide your light."*

He visualized the phenomenon that had unfolded during the night of fate. He repeated the scene several times to detect a clue. When leaving this trip, something caught his attention. The four asteroids of the four cardinal points had been extinguished one by one in a definite order. He remembered that the first to go out had taken the direction in which he had engaged. And that, this one was none other than the one with whom he conversed. He left this world and looked at the illuminated man still immersed in his book. He concluded that this was the first person to meet. Thus, he immediately deduced the second direction to be undertaken with his "ecoplasmic" echolocation guidance.

As if he had understood what was going on in the spirit of the Sufi, the enlightened man closed his book and spoke to him. "You finally found?"

He shook his head in affirmation.

"Among the servants, only scholars fear God," the illuminated said to him while getting up. To leave his element of always, the illuminated added, "Other information will be given to you by others." As he walked away, he added aloud, "He has the divine truth."

The Sufi watched him leave the place and disappeared behind the shrubs.

*How can such scholars, such sages, be ignored by a whole people? Certainly, they do not want to be discovered in order to avoid hindering their benevolence.* So monologued the Sufi.

The Sufi remained on the bench until dusk before returning.

*****

A few months later, the Sufi went to another continent. He attended a lecture of history in an amphitheater. At the end of the course, the students came out gradually. The professor seemed to linger to gather his stuff. When there remained only him and the Sufi, he finally raised his head toward his direction by speaking to him.

"Do you have questions?" asked the professor.

The Sufi went down a few steps to approach the professor. "I am on the quest for the guardian of the heavenly chest."

"Ah! I see. You too are on his quest! Only the most adventurous come to the point. His path is perilous, and his treasures cannot be limited in space or time.

A moment of silence, he packed his few belongings and sat comfortably on the desk before turning to the Sufi.

# The Heavenly Chest

In a parabolic language, the enlightened expressed itself. "The trunk, what a mystery! The manifestation of truth by truth. And who will tell you what it is?"

In his words, his gaze was lost in another dimension. Nostalgic, a moment later, he continued his narration with joy. "He was there when people were tearing each other apart. He will also always be there when these peoples disappear. He saw birth of multitudes civilizations. He also witnessed the disappearance of other achievements. However, there have always been people willing to give their lives to keep his secret."

He paused before resuming with a big puff of air testifying his pleasure to narrate. "In time immemorial, it was kept in the sanctuary of the divine, somewhere between the earth and the heavens, in the crossroads of the worlds, where a luminous ray crossing the heavens constantly came to pour out its quintessence.

A previous war, without respite, had opposed innumerable creatures coming from several worlds. Their goal was the chest, the famous mystery of tranquility. Each group wanted to monopolize it alone. Each of them thought they were the worthiest to keep the mystery because it was the source of the very essence of their existence. For some in the same world, it was necessary to keep the chest safe. For others, it was necessary to destroy it once and for all to end the existence and these interminable wars.

Alliances, plots, betrayals were made and defeated. Victories and defeats have been orchestrated in the different worlds. The fighting was raging. No world wanted to give in for fear of being annihilated by the other by its strategies of wars and wiles. It should be noted here that there were no referees. And there were no rules either. All shots were allowed. What mattered was the victory and to monopolize the trunk alone. No chance for mediation and no hope for peace!

At the edge of their total extinction, the sky rumbled! Divine grace was granted to them. A sanctuary was built, between the earth and the heavens, in the crossroads of worlds, where each people could finally contemplate it in its magnificence and recharge its elixir.

In the sanctuary, the chest was levitating, surrounded by a kind of fire without flame, a supernatural energy to avoid any direct contact. Even the most demonic creatures could not use their bodily fluidity to touch him because the energy around him was angelic.

Time had passed, and generations had evolved. But in what way?

In the sanctuary of the divine, evil spirits who wanted to steal the chest were always destroyed because it was protected by its own essence, a celestial vault. The wars of the worlds had considerably diminished, but that did not prevent some small groups from ever trying to take advantage of them. It had even become a warrior challenge to try to show his courage to his opponents. Despite multiple attempts, the chest was confined to its element.

The chest is a mystery. He defended himself. The code that allowed him to approach was lost in the bloody stride. The new generations also did not even know the existence of any code. They were content to contemplate it as their fathers and their fathers had done.

One day, a group of religious, who maintained the sanctuary and engaged in the aspiration of the knowledge of the mystery, ended up perceiving, in a transient way, the code written in figure of light on one of the facets of the chest. A moment later, the figure of light disappeared. It was the beginning of gnostic discoveries. These religious did not know the meaning of this symbol. Nevertheless, they now identified with this sign. They rushed to build similar metal symbols that they wore around their necks.

Centuries had passed without this mystery being deciphered, but they were passionate about the idea of trying. In addition, this sign was engraved on the most sacred object they claimed. No one, nor any creature, could appropriate it alone. Although called in different ways, in different worlds, this precious element was a common gift. For millennia, landscapes had changed without the sanctuary being changed from its original state. With the passage of time, the symbol worn by the descendants around their necks had lost its importance since nothing new had appeared. The very appearance of this symbol on the celestial chest became a myth.

One day, a monk who was cleaning up the shrine's outlines inadvertently murmured with an angelic voice, which has been kept secret from time immemorial, which has been erased from the minds of creatures who were tearing each other apart. Immediately, the trunk reacted with a sharp noise accompanied by luminescence. The symbol that the religious bore was immediately illuminated. The same symbol appeared in bright light on the six sides of the chest.

The person seemed to act in synergy with this famous chest. She was attracted to the trunk via her collar. The multicolored light was transferring into his collar before the chest was finally released from his levitation. The energetic vault that protected him disappeared as the trunk finally fell, and the ray of light coming from the sky became unnoticed. The monk hesitated to touch this mystery that no one, or any creature, had dared to touch before. Despite his resignation, the chest seemed to catch him. The light symbols on the trunk disappeared as the lid opened.

Astonishment!

Eyes wide open, the secret him, was manifested. He stood there, amazed, without a word to say. His discovery had mixed with a certain fright. He was now aware of why the chest was protected by angelic energy from its origin.

In a hurry, he tried to put the chest, levitated, but it fell with each attempt. He tried to forget everything to become as before, but with each effort, the secret resonated in his mind and was anchored more in his heart. He was trying to go back in time to find the trigger for this phenomenon. He tried to pronounce similar words, but nothing happened. The real word belonged to an angelic voice that could not come out of his mouth. Only a holy spirit could brave this dimension.

After a deep concentration, the word finally came out. Immediately, the symbol of his collar lit up, but the chest did not react. Thus, a luminous voice came from his necklace by a play of color. *"From now on, you are the guardian of the safe and its secret."*

A moment of stopping, then the luminous symbol continued, *"Wherever you are, you only need to hold the key to drink from all the powers and treasures of the world."*

This manifest voice had crossed the worlds. She had frozen everything that happened to hear him, like shaking earthquakes. Hordes of demons, who were busy with their daily tasks, were carefully fixed on these few vibrations. The universe resonated because the voice came from everywhere, and from nowhere.

From now on, they knew that the chest had been released from its protective vault, and that its secret was unveiled. There was also a so-called guardian. What was at the root of all the conflicts was once again arousing all the greed. The wars were going to become the daily life of the worlds again! Crowds across the worlds had abandoned their daily lives to indulge only in the quest for the safe and its guardian. Everything became as before, as their ancestors had reacted. Wars would certainly be raging. Militias began to organize themselves and the ancestral weapons out of their sheaths. Each armed himself with what he could. Hordes of demons began to gloat with their certainty of grabbing it while other creatures who heard the news were afraid of their future existence. In his worlds, the alliance with one of his adversaries is only a game of dupes.

Conscious of the danger he presented to the worlds, the guardian tried to attack his life to confirm the secret in his death. To the point of taking his own life, he glanced briefly at the chest, and the consciousness of not being able to protect him returned to him. He threw his weapon on the floor and finally came to take the chest with both hands. He huddled on the chest and sobs escaped him. He could not leave leaving the trunk defenseless, having lost his vault, and the only way to protect him was his collar activated by the key he was the only one to hold. It was immediately necessary to find a more secure place to hide the safe, but also to find people worthy of defending his secret against any evil spirit.

27

Some demons, thanks to their body fluidity, had managed to cross the borders of the telluric world. The guard had managed to gather around him, after some brief information, a small group of fortune composed mainly of his entourage and their family. Thus, began a long march toward lands hitherto unknown for the same cause, the defense of the celestial chest. They knew that this walk was not like the others because they certainly would not retrace their steps but also they risked losing their lives. There were a hundred to leave their village—men, women, children, and old men with their utensils.

In single file, they migrated immediately to distant horizons., crossing forests and tides, often under wind and rain. In this period of antiquity, only a few large cities were known. Sometimes, they were weeks away. They were mostly built as a fortress. It was common to see invaders come and try to annex these cities. With the experience of these attacks, the inhabitants had raised the walls, and barricades had been built all around. Hordes of ferocious beasts persisted in every country. Few people dared to venture into certain areas. With this insecurity evident outside the villages, brigands had formed to intercept the small groups in orde r to strip them before impaling them. Penitents and merchants from other cities also gathered in a large group of men and animals before leaving the city walls. The surrounding villages were frequently attacked until their destruction, either by raids or slavery. As a result, the few villages that existed were built in inaccessible natural areas.

The small group of guards and their families were determined to go as far as possible in the search for one of its natural interstices, where they could protect their burden. After a long walk, they found themselves in a swampy area. They settled on small islands of plots of land after having walked a lot in the swamp. In this expense, they hoped to find tranquility by isolation. Huts were erected on the par-cels of land that separated the puddles from the water. A larger box, where the chest was kept, was built in the middle of these dwellings. The presence of the chest in this lost area of nowhere had created a kind of harmony with nature. Everything was pushing easily. The game was within reach. Fish swarmed in the dripping waters. A kind of magnetism reigned. These invisible rays emitted by the chest were scented by demons from all walks of life. They sniffed the winds like a dog searching for prey.

At the zenith, a small group of demons had managed to locate and reach the site of the guards and their families. A fierce fight, without mercy, was delivered. Only adults had participated in this fight. The devils were easily defeated by the power of the symbols they wore on their necks. Initiates once knew how to activate them. As soon as he rested, another small group of demons appeared. They fought them to the last, but this time, there was a serious wounded among the guards.

At dusk, in the night and at dawn, the same scenes occurred. Thus, the guards agreed. They decided to look for another place where demons and evil people could not find them. The migration path was still resumed with an uncertain future. By twilight, a second group of more numerous incubators than the last had reached them. Like the previous fight, the guardian and his family exterminated them all, but with great difficulty. Two of them were killed, and three seriously wounded by the demons.

At night, a new demonic attack was wiped with great fright. Torches were lit all around the camp, and guards were ensured for the rest of the night.

Moons during, it was the same daily. Half of the initial group had been wounded, some of them having died, while the demons were becoming more and more numerous and more and more ferocious.

By dint of fighting all the time and without respite, they had become tired. The scars of bloody battles were read all over their bodies. They would spend three days and three nights of restless fighting before completely defeating a detachment of demons. They took the road of the exodus toward the East. They crossed a sandy plain, where they could be seen from afar. The great goalkeeper, who was behind all these journeys, urged them to go faster and to quickly leave the place where they were easily spotted for miles around.

Days had passed without meeting demons. Apparently, the movement of the chest prevented these evil creatures from orienting themselves through its angelic magnetism. A few days later, they found themselves in a valley where the rain was pouring over them. They were already wet to the bones as lightning struck a few meters from their positions. It was a question of taking refuge in a shelter for fear of being struck down. The roar of thunder so close was more frightening to the children. They immediately sought shelter where they would spend the rest of the shower.

A moment later, a cave was seen on the foothills of a mountain. They took the opportunity to take refuge and put a big warm fire. One of the guards took a torch from the fire and went closer to the wall, which he scanned. So he invited the great guard to come and see. Some of the guards approached. The light of fire revealed prehistoric drawings on the walls. Large game, including mammoths, were drawn on the walls. A landscape crowded with animals of all kinds was also included. Hunters held spears in different scenes.

A moment of admiration, one of the guards noticed a drawing similar to the landscape where they were, but without the animals. The foothills of the two mountains were drawn, and between which flocks of big game were hunted. The cave was well drawn on one of the foothills. An idea had just crossed the head of the great guardian. It was to paint their journey in the same cave to leave traces for future generations who will have the privilege of accessing this remote corner. He said to himself that certainly these drawings had crossed millennia. The abundant animals had disappeared from the landscape. The hunters too, but the place had remained in such a state as it was originally designed. A great artistic preparation was started fervently.

Moments later, they crushed coal to make a powder. Ashes were sifted. With the aid of the torches, they approached again the wall and drew their adventures. Different scenes could be observed. Scenes of fighting demons in the swamps. Scenes of steps in the sandy plains where appeared two characters holding the two opposite sides of the chest. And finally, a scene showing their arrival in the valley with lightning discharges.

The next day, at dawn, the rain had faded. The guards went out one by one, but a surprise awaited them. A horde of demonic creatures! They occupied the whole valley in close rows. Their rest in the cave had allowed the demons to detect and locate the chest. The place that seemed peaceful was alive, with a single shot of confrontation. A hubbub filled the landscape. Grunts of all kinds were emitted. The guards advanced a few steps in front of the entrance to the cave, followed by women, also armed, and children behind. The assault was given by the leader of the demons and his last swept over the guards, armed with their symbols around their necks, which they used as a weapon to explode. Before the first incubus reached the ranks of the guards, 96 percent of them were already killed. Close combat, sometimes in hand-to-hand combat, was delivered. The children took the opportunity to finish the demons in agony.

After bloody fighting, one of the guards was hit. The last of the devils was killed after an hour of fierce fighting. The killed guard was buried in front of the entrance to the cave. A large stone, on which was drawn the symbol, was placed on his tomb.

Moments later, the grand guard gave the order to leave before other hordes of demons arrived on the way. They continued their way to the east, where a chain of mountains stood before them. At mid-height, djebels up to the peaks were all white with snow, while their blankets were derisory. Nevertheless, they decided to cross this colossus. In any case they did not have much choice, either they would turn back and face the hordes of demons who were heading toward the place of the last signal emitted, the cave, or they would move in the freezing cold without much protection. Obviously! It was the last choice they had made.

When they were in the middle of the mountain, the hordes of demons were already at the level of the cave, but the location of the trunk was lost because of their movement. Some demons tried to desecrate the guardian's tomb, but the symbol engraved on the rock prevented them from digging it up. They began to run around the valley to find new traces in vain. At that moment, a snowstorm was blowing in the heights, with a violent wind, but that had not stopped the guards from rushing into the torment. They put themselves in a tight group to avoid the whips of the wind. The children and the women were placed in the center while the men exchanged positions in turn around the group. Their ordeal seemed endless. The pace was considerably reduced when the storm appeared. They finally camped on the spot and let themselves be covered with snow. The few objects they carried served to obstruct the passages of the wind, which seemed to tear their skins with thousands of small halberds. The children whined, the women groaned, and the men were content to reassure them with a better tomorrow. This rest time had alerted demons, who were now heading for their position.

A moment later, they were digging up a big snowball. The wind had already faded, and the landscape had calmed down again. The sky was clear, and the sun shone with thousands of rays. Aware of the danger, the grand guard gave the order to resume walking despite their fatigue and hypothermia. Legs staggered, bodies were arched, heads were down—the movement was negotiated and charges were barely fired. Their own bodies seemed to be burdened as they were determined to go to the end of their sentences as if their lives were meaningless without the trunk.

After their disappearance on the horizon, in relation to their encampment, some demons had managed to reach the camp, but the signal had disappeared since they were moving again. They searched for tracks in vain because the traces were immediately erased. The group of animals decided to split into several subgroups, each of which took a different direction to maximize their chances, while this option greatly reduced their assault power. Some individuals had taken the same track as that of the guards. They made a front toward a slope of a low mountain. The guards took the opportunity to exterminate them despite the harshness of the climate and the environment. The bodies were pushed into the precipices to prevent their congeners from finding traces. These battles seemed eternal!

The group of guardians, despite its small number, had the advantage, thanks to their pendants, whose meaning they did not know. They said they had faith and that the symbol was sacred because it had appeared in light on the treasure chest. Memories of the manifestation of the symbol on the chest had become vague. Several millennia had passed, but the new data experienced, by what they now called the great guardian and the liberation of the vault of his protective vault, made that they had fanned their faith to its paroxysm. They were ready to leave their lives there.

The descent was easier. It was enough to just slide down the slope, thanks to the snow that covered all surfaces.

*****

A moment later, they were on a less rugged area. They did not stop. All their needs were made in their movements. They had understood that inept people were attracted by the immobility of the trunk. After days of walking, they found themselves in a bamboo forest. To cross this landscape proved to be difficult. The obstacles were everywhere.

After so much effort, and in the middle of the forest, an idea crossed the head of the great guardian: to form a circle, where the women and children would be, to allow the group to rest. He told himself that bamboos would protect them against a massive attack. Nevertheless, the demons swept over them from all sides. They attacked each other in turn to fight them. Some were standing together while others were panting. The women came to clean the wounds and put on tourniquets while the children were drinking, but also, as usual, they also learned to exterminate the dying demons. The more they stayed on the spot to fight, the more demons became numerous. This did not solve their ordeal; on the contrary, the wounded became more and more frequent. Until then, they had not lost many men in the battles, but their forces had almost abandoned them. If it continued, they would still bury bodies. The great guardian again gave the order to move, fighting those who were already present. Their movements had allowed them to hide in the forest.

At this time, groups of chicks were already on the scene, but they could not locate them because the signal was gone. So one of the demon chiefs gave the order to burn the forest. The inflamed forest gave off a dense and asphyxiating smoke, which precipitated the small group in the disorder. The trunk and its secret would be lost forever by its carriers. It had been necessary for some good guards to turn back to get him out of the flames and carry him away. Three of them left their lives. The fiery forest kept them from continuing eastward, where the wind and the smoke were heading. They finally decided to take the direction of the north, which was more promising.

*****

As they walked, the tall trees disappeared, leaving the landscape to shrubs. Their movement was much easier. They were in a savannah. Herds of animals swarmed everywhere, allowing them to hunt and rebuild supplies. Still, they did not stop. They already knew the lesson. They had become unrecognizable, unlike their departure a few years ago. They did not shave, and they did not have spare clothes. Their clothes had become brownish rags. Some limped while others were mutilated. They had changed their rags with skins of big game. Some of them sported skins of zebras, wildebeest, or antelopes.

By dint of fighting all the time, they had reduced their diet considerably. Their main food came from hunting and gathering. The reserves barely kept for a few days. As a result, they formed a small group that went hunting as soon as possible. The direction of the caravan was given before the grooms so that they can find the traces of their congeners.

*****

The landscape had become bushy. The tall grass was golden, which was favorable to the wild beasts on the lookout, whose presence was unsuspected. The pack of lions charged the guards, confused with game that he used to hunt. Before understanding what was happening, two dead and three wounded were registered in their ranks. The beasts had ended up being pushed back with the hubbub.

Faced with this damage, they hastened to leave the tall grass.

*****

The landscape became more and more arid. Certainly, the desert was announced. Instead of trees and shrubs, there were acacias and clumps of thorny plants. The ground became more and more bare. It was the steppe.

*****

The sand dunes were in sight as they left behind the steppe. They hesitated to turn back, but the big guard convinced them to continue since it was their destiny. He said to himself, "If we must die, why not be so by defending this precious object?"

Thus, the desert was trampled, but they completely ignored its extent. They also said to themselves, "We are guided by our faith."

Days of walking in this monotonous expanse, and half of them left life there. Water and food were missing. The physical effort in this environmental hostility had reduced them into skeletons. The sky wore rainy clouds, which only happened once or twice a year in this desert. The sun was momentarily hidden, thus providing a little respite from gray, where the humidity of the air was zero. The hope of being wet gave them a boost of strength to stand up again.

A dilemma arose: if they stopped, the demons would locate them and end up killing them all and recovering the chest; if they continued, they would certainly die of hunger and thirst. And in the end, the demons would locate the chest and end up looking for it without a fight. They chose to die fighting.

A time of rest, then the dunes of sand were filled with demons. The guards immediately went into concentric circles. Seen from the sky, it gave the appearance of a gigantic eye, within the center, the small group of guardians representing the iris, around them, the portions of sand were still not occupied by the attackers, and finally, the demons overhung all dunes, representing the cornea.

Given the number of demons that were present on the scene and the exhaustion that was on the face of the guards, the fight was lost in advance. From all sides, these evil creatures swept over them. A fierce battle was fought. Children and women, who were usually protected by men, all started fighting. Despite the descent of countless attackers before their arrival on the small group, the demons had finally reached them. The fight had become a melee. The chest remained the focal point of their defense. The exhaustion of the guards played to their disadvantage. The small concentric group at the beginning gradually became dislocated. Thus, they fell one by one under the assault.

Close to their complete annihilation, the crash! Thunder rose from the sky! Suddenly, they stopped fighting. The animals seemed to be terrified by this unexpected new situation in this desert expanse. They submitted—with their backs bent, heads bowed, and some eyes riveted upward. Something in the sky scared them. Some demons abandoned the fighting and tried to retreat by fleeing, while others were paralyzed by terror.

A curtain of water droplets was moving toward them. Something that brought salvation to the guards became a nightmare for the demons. The rainwater ran through them like rifle bullets. Despite their speed of flight and their disparate nature, they all ended up being overtaken by this blessing. The group of guards of a hundred people—initially composed of men, women, children and old men—was reduced to about twenty unrecognizable ghosts. They sprawled on the ground and let themselves be soaked by providence. Some took the opportunity to quench their thirst by simply opening their mouths.

For long hours, the rain fell on them. Without moving the chest, they did not observe demons on the horizon. Water infiltrated instantly into the ground. Nevertheless, they put their flasks back to full. The rain had led to the digging up of the few desert animals. Immediately, they began to eat insects and arachnids to restore energy. The meat of the vipers and small lizards served as dried reserves for the rest of the crossing. From now on, they had additional information about the demons. They were afraid of the blessed water.

At the end of the rain, they started walking again to avoid attracting new villains. This intervention reassured them more than ever about the nobility of their mission. They continued in the same direction, hoping to meet the sea where water is out of sight, the best refuge against their enemies.

*****

After a few days of walking, a wet breeze finally brushed their faces. They knew now that the sea was not far away. A moment later, they already saw gulls overhanging them. A little later, they had finally reached the sea. They walked along the coast to find a passage. They seemed to get a break by the ocean. For months they had not been attacked. This peaceful state gave them satisfaction. They concluded that the water, in addition to being harmful to these demons, could also blur their bearings. They took the opportunity to regain strength, with the crustaceans crawling along the beaches, and fill their food reserves.

Since they had begun their journey, years had passed. They had seen people who were dear to them disappear. Children were born while the original population was aging. They knew that these battles could not last forever. Their ranks dwindled while those of the demons seemed to be inexhaustible. It was necessary to find a durable solution before their extinction, or their corruption by the adventures.

On a cliff, they saw a small boat stranded on a sandy bay. They rushed down the heights, slipping on steeper slopes. The wooden vessel was probably abandoned long ago because of its dilapidated state. The coral began to take hold of it. Large parts of planks were already gnawed by the weather. All around, they found countless remains of similar ships, utensils, rust-ridden weapons, and planks hidden everywhere. It looked like an old landing place for an ancient army, or an old battleground between different warring fleets. They had found a trick for a time of respite. It was enough to wade a few meters and keep the trunk in the ship. Thus, the sea was used to scramble the tracks.

Days had passed, and the environment had changed as well. Thus, they learned to swim and fish. This gave them plenty of protein and fat. However, the area was low in foliage when they had to balance their diet with plant to obtain sugars for metabolic energy, but also vitamins essential for the proper functioning of their bodies.

The first goalkeeper became very old when he was the only one to get in touch with the trunk. His worries grew on the future of the chest after his death. After long reflections and moments of loneliness, an idea crossed her head. It was to repair the boat with the debris of planks abandoned on the beach. They undertook a major renovation project.

A few moons later, the boat floated again. They went to sea without a specific destination. They sailed under the influence of the winds and headed south. However, they tried not to get too far off the coast. After moons of navigation, the boat hit a coastal rock. The port side was torn off, and sinking was inevitable. They all swam toward the shore.

Weakened by the stigma of time and fighting, the guards no longer had much hope for a new place of refuge. The area where they capsized did not have many trees to rebuild any raft.

In a sunny day, when the sky was bare of clouds, the great guardian entered into communication with the trunk. He was surprised by this extremely rare phenomenon. The chest announced his impending death. He also gave him a solution to better preserve his secret for the sake of his congeners, but also a mercy for the worlds. It was a question of pronouncing the supreme word and ordering the chest to choose one of his most worthy to be his successor. Without delay, the grand guard made the trunk's advice. Immediately, the box became translucent and disappeared into the body of one of the guards who inherited all the essence and hidden knowledge.

The next day, the great guardian gave up the ghost. At the same moment, all the waves that attracted the demons disappeared. Suddenly, the worlds seemed to darken. This state froze the creatures in a sort of imminent announcement that was soon to be read on the faces. The crib had just been hidden. Henceforth, he could no longer be contemplated in his original state, and only very rare among them could perceive his glimmers. His name had only become murmur in the hearts of holy spirits because those of the shadows, not knowing where to look, had developed their eyes and their ears to intercept the slightest whistling of the winds.

From generation to generation, the maie chose his host to spread his essence in hearts yearning for peace. It was called The Hidden or The Concealed. He is the guide who advances the worlds because he is the origin and the judicious explanation of the apparent world. He is the quintessence of the lights concealed from all knowledge.

This lord could be anyone. He could be a prince, like a slave; a rich man, like a poor man; a big man, like a child; an old man, like a child; and a White man, like a Black man. It could also be anywhere in any part of the world. His name was The Clairvoyant.

For centuries, the demons who searched for the chest had been annihilated at zero. Their disparate nature hardly allowed them to locate it. Thus, they tried to possess human bodies to reach their end.

*****

At the end of his narration, the illuminated man gave a great sigh as if he had just freed himself from a heavy burden. He finally turned his head slightly toward the Sufi. The two eyes met without a word to say.

A moment later, the professor continued. "And what did you get from the chest?" asked the illuminated.

"That it is a hidden treasure belonging to all the creatures of the worlds."

"And?"

"And that the ancients sacrificed themselves for us to inherit. It is up to us to be sure in their footsteps in order to be merciful to the worlds."

Thus, the illuminated man raised his head as an affirmation. However, the Sufi asked a question. "And what's in the heavenly chest?"

"Mystery! All that I can say, which can only be murmured by pure hearts, is because it is at the center of all forms of understanding and meaning, like a perfectly straight path through which the majestic realities are manifested."

The professor got up from the desk, waved, and patted him on the shoulder. He took his things and encouraged him in these terms. "The path is dangerous. Only scientists can endure his adventures. You need the star of knowledge because it is the lantern to guide yourself."

This corresponded to the same terms as the onrocriticism he had consulted since the beginning of his quest and the first star. Part of his mystery seemed to be resolved, but he had to find the other two stars to complete his guidance. He needed knowledge, such were the words of his scholars.

A dilemma imposed itself. That would mean that despite all he had acquired during his many journeys, he knew nothing! He had had recurring dreams, and he had consulted a specialist scholar. The latter had told him about the night of fate. After so much effort and observation, providence had given him the opportunity to detect his signs, which he had doubtless followed and which allowed him to narrowly avoid a bicycle in the dark, to avoid their vehicle crashing against a truck without taillights and parked in the middle of the road. His visit to an initiatory master allowed him to move from the normal view to the infrared view, then from the thermal to the ultra-violet view. Thus, he had found the first star and then the second. Nevertheless, they repeated to him the same thing: "*To go to the quest for knowledge.*"

After the professor's departure, he remained meditative for a moment, alone in the amphitheater.

Ideas crossed his head. *If a lot of guardians, in spite of their protective pendants, were killed by the demons, how would I deal with an attack?*

His questions were, without second thoughts, without answers. He did not know. Thus, the words of the scholar came back to him: "*Being aware of one's ignorance is the first step toward knowledge.*"

He smiled a smile on his lips as if everything was mystery. He stood there for a moment, looking out at the empty seats in the amphitheater before leaving in search of the other two stars, whose geolocations were continental.

# Demonic Possession

Cries came from the neighbor's house. For three weeks, nobody could sleep. From time to time, broken porcelains, glasses against the wall, utensils, din, insults, everything was there. The house was becoming more and more popular with family members. Everyone was trying to bring a grain of consolation to the stricken family. Their only daughter was seriously ill. It was a girl—calm, humble, who did not go out much. She was shy. She did not look at people in the eyes, a simple girl without stories.

Nobody knew what had happened to her. It was madness. Sometimes she calmed down, and sometimes she struggled in the hands of her parents who tried to hold her so that she did not destroy the few goods they had left. She was quarantined with fear, she was thought to have rabies, but the retention time was well above that of the rhabdovirus incubation. The cries of dementia were similar, but she did not have the phobia of the water as with the madmen. It did not drool, either; all the other clinical signs were obvious.

After six months of quarantine, and without improvement, a caravan had brought her to a city at the desert gate where she was finally interned in the psychiatric hospital. Without spoiling the latter, it was a little house where they kept some mentally ill.

She, who was shy now, insulted everyone. Her parents were not left behind. The more shocking the insult, the more satisfied she was. It happened to her to search for the most vexing words. She could use a word and then go back and consider that the word insulting was not enough. Her parents could no longer afford psychiatric care, which was expensive and brought her home.

Despite all that was spent, she could not find an improvement in her condition. On the contrary, the evil had worsened. Not only did she insult everyone, she broke everything, but also undressed in front of everyone. It looked like her clothes burned her body. Without further solutions, her parents were advised to bring her to the witch doctor.

All tracks were borrowed without good results. Some said she was possessed by the devil. This was confirmed by the sheer force she possessed during the trance parties. She managed to project everyone who was holding her in one movement. Thus, she took the opportunity to undress naked when she was only twenty-three years. Her modesty of entant was forgotten.

Endowed with an insurmountable force, she was finally bound, hands and feet, by her parents. See the scene, we would wonder if her family was indeed human. A question arose: How can you tie your child like an animal?

She seemed to become lucid only when she was tied up. She spoke well. She stopped insulting. She reasoned about her situation. She made promises not to do it again.

After long moments of mastery, she begged them to detach her. Her supplications were heard to the street. She cried. She was suffocating. She simulated moments of agony. Each time, her parents attended scenes of their child's death, which was unbearable. Thus, the paternal and maternal instinct prevailed over their reason. She finished being detached but immediately began her trances. She immediately lost her memory and then sank back into madness.

People were desperate. Nobody knew what it was. Adequate solutions seemed nonexistent.

One evening, when everyone was at the neighbor's house and his father was not back from the caravan yet, Makham, the five-year-old, did not fail to follow his mother to the neighbor's house. It was a new crisis scene. She was in a trance. She insulted everyone, but a presence seemed to bother her. She tried to find her by staring at people, but each time, she gave up, as if that presence was stronger than her.

The house was a little dark; the faces of people poorly lit. At each attempt, she retreated immediately with frightful fear. She seemed to be curbed by an invisible barrier. It was a new attitude. She would run for shelter, where she huddled, as if something were chasing her.

Moments later, curiosity dominated her. She retraced her steps to identify the people in the yard. The scene was repeated dozens of times. Each time, it was the same reaction. Everyone had noticed these new things that were becoming the new topic of conversation.

Since no one knew what had happened to her despite multiple consultations everywhere, from modern medicine to traditional medicine, one was content to comment on her reactions.

"Finally, something scares her!" Some murmured.

The onlookers, not knowing what it was, still rejoiced at this unusual situation that prevented her from trying to escape from the house. She was no longer trying to get out of the house; rather, she was staring at people. She was now fast and left with her demons. Seeing no one cared for her anymore, she changed tactics. She knew that her actions did not affect anyone. Seeming no longer to flee, hindered by something, she undressed naked like a worm. People tried not to look at her. Now it was throwing stones and utensils. Everyone was running away, trying to escape. She was trying to get out of the house again but always turned back. Something scared her. However, she continued her throws. She was immediately mastered on the ground. She does not break out as usual. On the contrary, she tried to stare at the people who mastered her. Her position on the ground did not allow her to see them all. In a calm and serene voice, she asked to be allowed to watch one of the people holding her feet. Her aggressive attitude had deeply changed. She had returned to normal, but people did not want to run the risk of giving her time to regain her enormous strength.

Nevertheless, some people let go, but she did not seem to find any strength to get up. It was at that moment that she specified her intention to look only at the person holding her right foot. It turned out, he was a child! Thus, she uttered a peaceful and sad tone.

"I beg you. I only want to know who is holding my right foot. He has infinite strength. I can not fight him."

She was convincing since she could not move from her position, although some would have let go. Little by little, suspiciously, people released her. She slowly and respectfully sat down. Now everyone had let go, except Makham, the five-year-old. A little astonishment was visible in his eyes.

"Ah! It's our neighbor's child!" Respectfully, she spoke to him.

"Forgive me. I will not disturb anymore."

The child behaved strangely. He set himself in a dominant position and seemed to know the suffering of the young woman.

"It's time for you to stop obsessing my loved ones."

The girl seemed to obey by the head. So everyone was surprised at his behavior. She, who had no shame before anyone, bowed before a child!

"Yes. If you let me go, I will not come back. I will leave them alone."

"No. I'm going to send you where you are from."

Fright was in her voice and in her eyes. Certainly, she did not expect this situation.

"No! Everything but that! No!"

Makham did not answer. However, the young woman continued her entreaties before the five-year-old. Something new was emerging in the atmosphere. Thus, people retreated little by little in front of this situation. A smile could be seen on Makham's lips. Immediately, the voice of the young woman accelerated with great dismay. Excruciating cries were uttered.

"No! No! Nooooooooon!"

She became stiff after a long scream. Immediately, his father tried to revive her. In a waving hand, he was immediately prevented by the young child. He did not let go of the fainting woman's feet.

A moment later, the child made a diversion. He behaved as if nothing had happened. He finally released the woman and immediately became a mere child, seeming to be frightened by the behavior of the young woman. He ran to snuggle between the legs of the young woman's father. Innocently, he showed a misunderstanding of the young woman's behavior. This unexpected posture surprised everyone again. People had seen him converse with the young woman until she fell, fainting. He pointed his index finger at the dead body, addressing the young woman's father.

"She liked to fool people! She liked to deceive people!"

The diversion seemed to work. Immediately, people forgot what had happened. They ran to master her before she got up again and became elusive.

After being mastered, she slowly opened her eyes. Her eyes were wide open in astonishment. She immediately spoke. "But! What are you doing to me?"

She addressed everyone through her name. "Why do you control me on the ground? What do you have? Are you crazy or what?"

Everyone knew that something had changed. She had never spoken to people like that since the beginning of her illness. She was immediately released. She stood up with shame at seeing herself completely undressed. She kept wondering what had happened and why everyone was gathered in their house.

Reading the people's eyes, she felt she was not normal. Shame assaulted her. She took refuge in her room. Surprisingly, she was cured.

A few days later, after her parents told her about what had happened, she did not want to leave the house. The shame of insulting her parents did not vanish from her memory. Nobody knew what had healed her. People were not even paying attention to the latest behaviors with Makham. A five-year-old boy, who behaved in the same way as most children his age, might not attract attention, especially when it came to the banal neighbor.

Despite everything that had happened, nothing had changed in Makham's life. He laughed like everyone else and continued to play with his friends.

# The Unconsciousness of the Risks

As usual, Makham crouched on the highest dune overlooking the oasis with a look lost in the desert, in search of the arrival of a caravan. However, the other children played different games. He was always the first to warn others about such an arrival. These moments were always a party. In a short time, the voices took turns, and the whole village echoed the echoes of such an arrival. People were quick to mass on the main market square. It was a great opportunity for some to see their husbands, their fathers and uncles, but also to get new information about distant lands. Recent goods were soon examined. Some caravans could line up several hundred loaded dromedaries. Of course, the flow of these goods required several months, but the people rushed to be the first served. These convoys were the only means of contact with the so-called civilized world, and it was not common to find one. Months could happen before such fullness. A new energy could live in the oasis for several days. Everyone wanted to find his account because the desert was unpredictable, and the early signs of the fondouks did not announce such monsoons bringing rain.

On the dune, Makham was trying to pierce the horizon. It even happened that he announced the imminent arrival of a caravan while the watchers could not see anything. Sometimes, it took three more hours for lookouts before seeing a small black spot in the horizon, designating the trailer. Often, some of his comrades asked him how he did to find out, but he always replied, "I see them coming."

His ignorance of his providential abilities did not allow him to explain his understanding. He thought that everyone was like him, and that it was enough to look to see.

For two hours, his act of scrutinizing the mirages gave him nothing, sand only sand. Suddenly, a small hand held his. It was one of his friends who wanted to invite him to go to the lake for a swim. The oasis was in a shallow bottom near the water table. It hardly rained all year-round, but this place still had open water. The depth of the lake could reach several meters and engulf adults who could not swim.

It was common for parents to prohibit their children from venturing there. Nevertheless, some stubborn young people went there and ended up knowing how to swim, despite the few tragic cases of drowning. The turbid water played little for the drowned. Once disappeared in the water, the body could be found only after regurgitation by the lake—no doubt a certain death and sometimes a beginning of putrefaction. Sometimes parents would tell fables about the lake or evoke tragic memories to deter their children.

It was not a favorite place for Makham. The few rare cases where he went there, he always put himself on the bank, watching his friends play. Date palm fields bordered the coast. In the middle of the lake, a hundred meters from the bank, stood a small island of sand emerged. Despite the distance and the depth of several meters, the children defied themselves to be the first to arrive. It was trivial for them, this kind of game.

On the shore, he held the few clothes of his friends, watching them swim like fish. Not being innate, swimming required several learning sessions. Not only did you have to know how to swim but also have an athletic background to get there.

A moment later, one of his elders of more than three years came to dissuade him from going to soak. Makham declined the offer, but the latter persisted in assisting him in case of problems.

"Come, I'll teach you how to swim," his friend told him.

"I never swam," replied Makham.

"Do not be afraid. We are all crossing. It's not difficult. You just have to want it and swing your arms."

The same answer came back to him, "I never swam."

After several invitations, he yielded and finally undressed by having faith in his host. The unconsciousness of the risks did not tingle in their heads because of their young age. Makham was five years old and the other was eight. Having never saved someone from drowning, and even having never seen such an opportunity, he certainly could not save him in a disaster. He only thought that it was enough to be at his side, and the rest was played.

They stepped into the water, soaked, then Makham stopped. He paused. He hesitated a moment, and his intuition convinced him to succeed. He continued to his knees, and the same experience was repeated. He walked to the chest, and it was always the same. So, always at his side, his friend invited him to float on the water, and he executed like a soldier in front of his captain.

They began to swim. The distance separating them from the islet gradually diminished. A moment later, they were on the block. Time passed, but Makham did not want to return to the mainland. The instinct that animated him seemed to leave him. The fear of failure overwhelmed him, despite the same encouragement of his friend.

Hours passed, but he did not want to leave the island. In a moment, his mother, as animated by a sixth sense, jumped suddenly and worried about the absence of his son. She looked for him in the various places of games in vain. She called him loud, but no one answered his call. At the same time, in his encampment on the islet, his mother's voice sounded satiated; as usual, his young age did not allow him to distinguish these extremely rare facts.

Rich people could afford with all their wealth to acquire this subtle knowledge that was the subject of bloody wars between different worlds. Hordes of demons had been slaughtered because of this precious thing, the secret of power that was in the trunk of which he kept the key. He was wanted everywhere while he was confined in the desert, in a small oasis lost in the middle of nowhere. He rushed. He forgot his fear, and his carelessness guided him back into the water.

Faster than his friend, he arrived at the shore while the latter was halfway through the distance.

# Makham and the Little Sparrow

Most of the able-bodied men had gone on caravans, while at that time, women were engaged in housework. Small children like Makham played to build castles with the fine sand of the desert.

At one point, one of the children invited the others to pick up the few dates, which had fallen on the ground, in the plantations. Indeed, the desert aspect of the surroundings was hardly in the oasis. In addition to the lake, there was a fertile area of about one square kilometer in which date palms naturally grew.

The desert was huge, while there were no water points hundreds of miles away. This biotope contrasted with that of the desert. The few species of desert birds found refuge there. With the presence of water, food, and shade, the birds there proliferated.

At dawn, the wild rhythm of the cries of the chicks sang a harmonious melody that lasted until dusk. They were born in the oasis, grew up in this small piece of land, and then died. None of them had the strength to brave this monotonous expanse. Children used to hunt them with slingshots, and this allowed them to eat poultry frequently.

Makham, accompanying the other children, most of whom were older than him, was walking in the woods. They picked up dates. Suddenly, Makham froze without moving. He turned his attention to something.

A moment later, he imitated the cries of the birds. His friends were amazed at this ability because of his very young age because they were unable to do so. Everyone approached him to listen to him.

A moment later, one of his friends held his hand and spoke to him. "How are you doing this?"

"I was chatting with a chick." And it was hilarity.

"The birds do not understand us. We are talking. They are singing," another said.

"Yes, yes. He understood me."

"How did he understand you? What was he saying?"

"He said he had been waiting for his mother for two days and had not eaten anything yet."

And it was still the laughs. Thus, Makham stopped these jokes.

"Listen. Listen."

He started whistling again, then the chick answered him like that. He intoned another melody, and it was the same. The children did not believe their eyes. Some tried to try the experiment, but the chick did not answer. They imitated a lot of hissing of other birds, and it was the same silence.

They asked Makham to start again. It was not long to amaze them again. Thus, they understood the harmony that reigned between the two interlocutors. However, they did not accept Makham's words of understanding the chick and being understood by this creature. In this respect, the ears were directed toward the slightest whistling of the birds. They retried the experience with the other birds but did not find a return.

Makham pointed to the nest perched on a branch. Everyone froze without waiting.

A moment later, they continued on their way. After filling their saddlebags with these succulent fruits, the children turned back. At the same spot, Makham rushed to the bottom of the tree trunk where the nest of the chick had perched. He picked up a little sparrow whose sleeping clothes had just begun to come out.

"How did you come down?" Makham asked him.

"I fell."

"Did you fall alone? It must hurt!"

"Staying here means certain death as I felt you approaching again."

"Now how am I going to do it?"

"Take me with you."

"If my friends find you, they will eat you."

"Say it's a baby sparrow, and they could not share it."

"So what? They eat birds of all ages."

"Ask them to wait until I'm an adult to be consistent."

At this moment, one of the children approached and saw Makham carry his hand from behind to hide something.

"Show me," he ordered the child.

He reached out his arm and slowly opened his hand. The child was quick to alert others. Everyone came to see the catch, but the report was disappointing. The prey was too thin. Proposals on the purpose of the fledgling were made instantly, but Makham answered them by remembering the words of the fledgling. They agreed to wait until he was an adult. They thus forgot that the sparrow could hardly exceed an inch even at adulthood, but their dream of a great feast overcame their knowledge.

Makham undertook to be the breeder of the chick since it was he who had picked it up, which did not lead to opposition. When he arrived home, he found his mother pounding the grain. He told his story to his mother, and she did not want to confuse him in his imaginary world and encouraged him to raise him. He took some grain seeds, chewed them, and spat them in his hand before handing them to the sparrow. The latter swallowed with a few pecks and was finally saved from hunger.

Days passed, then the sparrow filled up. Where people had dogs and cats as pets, Makham was content with a sparrow. From now on, he never left his *adoptive father*, who seemed to be overjoyed to feed him and to discuss with him. Sometimes, he was hopping on his shoulders, sometimes on his head. Sometimes, he landed on his lips and pecked at him some grain seeds in his mouth. The sparrow, now able to fly, went to the plantations to report stories to Makham, which further refined his knowledge of the bird world.

One day, the sparrow was slow to return, and the child was worried about his future. There was no more than an hour in the woods, but this time he was away all day. Makham did not see him come back and abstained from lunch, despite repeated invitations from his mother. The same scene was repeated at the afternoon snack, which consisted of serving the remains of the breakfast to the children.

Makham sulked all food and went camping at the entrance to the village. His mother came to hold his hand and promised to buy him a rooster, but Makham did not want it. According to him, he had promised Yakhar, the sparrow, to serve him the two seeds of peanuts he had reserved for him. Thus, his mother did not understand why his son was stubbornly keeping his promise to a chick.

In the face of this extremely rare behavior of a five-year-old child, a dilemma settled in his mother's head. Bring the child forcibly home and then push him to break one of the great virtues, the respect of the promise, or leave him in the twilight to wait for a chick who ignores the world of men. His mother finally stood beside him, staring at the woods. And time passed.

The solar disk was beginning to sink in the sunset. At the last ray of the sun, everyone had to return to the houses, because in this culture of the desert, the Djinns, having no place to go in this monotonous expanse, were heading toward the oasis.

Some said that the first inhabitants of the oasis were the Djinns, then the humans came to dislodge them. Thus, a great war had settled between the two groups. With a lot of casualties on both sides, a former great sage who came to see the Djinn in their world began negotiations. The inhabitants concluded, thus, that the day was for the humans and the night for these spirits. For them, twilight and dawn were the barriers of both worlds.

Fables circulated and told different meetings that did not always end in the cordial agreement. It was not uncommon to see someone possessed by demons and to have reproached himself for having forgotten this pact between the two species.

*"You are so used to seeing only beings dressed in matter that you cannot see beings in light or in etheric energy,"* accused the old sage of the oasis.

In addition to the delimitation of time, it was forbidden to pour hot water on the ground, to speak too loudly at night, and many other instructions that regulated the understanding of the two worlds. To see the immense joy that the company of the sparrow provided to his son and the distress of the moment, the sadness could be read on the face of the mother, who now looked at the woods, sometimes at her son.

At the last glimmers of hope, the sparrow came from the woods, and it was jubilation. The child could no longer restrain himself. His mother's face became radiant again. However, the sparrow came to rest on his head, alternated both shoulders as usual, then he tried to peck saliva on his mouth to greet him. Thus, the child forgot his pain and returned with his mother in the house, just at the disappearance of the sun.

It was a long conversation about his absence.

"When I went to inspect the woods, I witnessed a great fight between different bird clans," said the sparrow.

"Quarrels!"

"Yes, arguments. They fought for the best place in the woods."

"And why did you last so long?"

"After months of battles, they finally agreed to set up an assembly to decide between them, but a problem arose. None of the belligerents wanted a judge from the opposing camp when there were no others. In the end, they had agreed to be judged by the first intruder. Weeks had passed, and they found hardly any judge. Seeing me enter the woods, everyone rushed to me. They had kept me so that I could decide between them."

"And their territories they claimed?"

"They had left them going until I arrived. None of them had the right to enter. They were looking for food in the vicinity, but this task was dangerous for them because there is only this area other than the desert. During all this time, they had held me back. It had been necessary to listen to all the witnesses before deciding. They told me that their previous talks had not resulted in a consensus because everyone wanted to hunt in the morning, which was the best time."

"After, what did you decide?"

"Listening to them, I concluded that none of them could appropriate it alone. They could not prove their creation of this place, or their heritage vis-a-vis a local creator. So to avoid hurting such and such, I decided that the place belongs to all."

"How's that? And if they could not stick to it all at the same time?"

"I decided that from noon until the next day at the same time, a group will stay there. And then in turn, each group can finally hunt each day. It will be able to enjoy every hour without them meeting in the same place."

"You have been wise. Where did this knowledge come from?"

"I was inspired by your agreement with the Djinns who govern the night and the humans during the day. My adoption by humans has allowed me to acquire this wisdom."

Suddenly, Makham seemed to remember something. He took two peanut seeds out of his pocket, which he crushed with his teeth and then spat in his hand, which made the sparrow excited. He handed it to him before uttering, "You see. I held my promise."

The sparrow was soon pecking his meal.

The village became darker and darker. The custom was once again respected.

# The Desert and its People

A three-day walk from the oasis was a rock salt mine. It was an old prehistoric sea that had dried up. After the disappearance of the water, the salt that had dissolved had crystallized. Thus, forming a compact mass of salt several meters thick to several kilometers in diameter.

The artisanal exploitation of salt went back several generations. Salt-plating techniques were handed down from father to son. Thus, caravans were made of dromedaries each loaded six blocks of about twenty kilos toward some major sub-Saharan cities.

Makham's father was part of a team of about ten people lining up 212 animals. The trip could last several months before returning to the village. Most of the inhabitants of the oasis had never left this desert world. The caravans were always greeted with great enthusiasm because their arrival meant a great supply of goods and information. It was the only umbilical cord that tied them to the rest of the world. The inexistence of villages, or nearby towns, for some exchange had sunk the oasis in a time standstill. The same landscape had not changed much for centuries. The only resources were derived from the sale of dates and the exploitation of the Gemme salt mines. What was only routine had frozen time in a medieval world.

Makham's father was back in the oasis after several months of absence. Makham had just celebrated his fifth birthday two weeks earlier. So his father promised to bring him on his next trip. It is customary for this people to introduce children to their father's work as early as their fifth year. In this respect, he was excited by the idea of discovering other horizons.

After a few days' stay, his father returned to the desert respecting his promises. They went to the salt mine. His father invited him to come up to him and observe how he was doing to get out well-cut blocks of salt. After several weeks in the mine, the caravan was loaded with salt. They now headed to the first big cities at the door of the Sahara.

Timbuktu, "the city of the 333 saints," or otherwise "the pearl of the desert," was their destination. This city, founded in the fifth century, was in the Middle Ages—a city of intellectual and spiritual knowledge. In these modern times, more than one hundred thousand manuscripts dealing with several sciences and literatures are enumerated. The city, with its multitude of schools and medieval mosques, is classified World Heritage by UNESCO.

# The Tea Ceremony

I n the Timbuktu market square, the caravan unloaded the blocks of salt it had transported for more than a thousand kilometers. The negotiations were based on ancestral Bedouin codes, although religion was rooted in these populations. In times of scarcity of certain commodities, it was common to see caravans intercepted even before arriving at the marketplace, but the code prohibited any sale. The sale was to be auctioned, and only on the marketplace.

The caravan was soon sold because the salt was missing for days. The camels were brought to specialized places so that they could drink.

A dispute arose between the caravaneers and a merchant. Indeed, the trader reproached the caravaneers for having erred on the count of salt blocks. The latter refuted such accusations. The caravaneers argued on the number of 212 dromedaries, each of whom carried six blocks of salt, but the shopkeeper counted less. Nobody could decide between them because the camels were already displaced. They did not know if the missing came from before or after the sale of salt. At one point, a few onlookers surrounded them.

After a long interaction, to bring back peace, it was Makham's father who suggested to the trader to cut the missing out of his hand. This dilemma of justice will traverse the city to the ears of the great scholar of the city. He greatly appreciated the caravaneer's gesture. Without delay, he sent an emissary to invite him to attend his tea ceremony. Among these desert peoples, tea occupied a rather important place. The best thing to honor a guest is to share tea with him. It was a moment of predilection to discuss around the murmurs of the desert.

The great scholar was the imam, the preacher, and the judge. His assemblies never lacked crowds. They listened to him, and they admired him. His fame had already gone through huge areas. People referred to him for many religious decisions. Approaching it was a great privilege. To be invited by him was the greatest honor a Bedouin could have.

An individual brought them a camel-skinned mat, on which they sat next to the great scholar. The great learned thus began his sermons under the attentive ear of his disciples. He spoke of equity in transactions.

A moment later, and in full sermon, Makham rose from the mat and joined the scholar who did not fail to welcome him. The event was rare because children were not allowed in these kinds of assemblies. However, the great scholar did not interrupt his speech.

As time went on, suddenly, something seemed to attract the scholar's attention to Makham. He was silent, still staring at the child. Time passed without the notable changing of his state.

Telepathically, Makham began a conversation.

"You will leave in a week."

"Where to go?" asked the scholar.

"On the other side. The beings of heaven are satisfied with you."

"So are you the one I was waiting for?"

Makham shook his head in acquiescence, without uttering a word.

"Finally, I found it! God be praised," continud the enlightened.

The scientist's eyes sparkled with mysteries before he turned again to the assembly. He immediately changed his speech.

"I will tell you the story of the last day of Komalo," said the scholar.

This turn of events gave rise to a few whispers before the scholar began to narrate.

# The Last Day of Komalo

Komalo was a trader. He was like most of his peers. He had an active life full of enthusiasm. He had always sought, throughout his life, to earn money to get rich. He had fought. He had quarreled. He had to go. He was wrong, but above all, he had no sense for his life.

What does it matter how important his visions are? He lived as he had seen his fathers live. Questions in oneself were not welcome. Unthinkable to question anything about his life, he had tried to take advantage of it, but hey, one of his problems was that he did not know how to discern the usefulness of futility.

In the long run, it had become a puzzle. He was content to live, and that was all. He was not planning for the long-term. He lived from day-to-day. He could strive to get something by not sleeping, by depriving himself of all other pleasure, by being stressed, and by combining all his efforts just for this purpose. After the latter's attack, he found himself discouraged to have spent all his time seeking futility. It became a heavy burden because his taste dried up very quickly. It looked like it was not the goal of his fury.

He found himself looking for other things without asking questions. He quickly forgot his disappointment and started again with the same behavior. So on, he had spent all his life regretting without questioning himself for fear of discovering a law that would incite him to change his behavior, that of everyone, and that of his fathers.

In his childhood, he was only trying to become an adult. All his dreams were oriented in this direction. It was his ultimate wish. He became a teenager; he only wanted to get married. That was the meaning of his life: *find a beautiful woman*. After getting married, some time later, he found himself in unparalleled trouble. Never during his life had he endured so much reproach, jealousy, and constant surveillance. To stifle this monotony, he looked for children who could understand him. There, he could not anymore because the charges and the problems multiplied. In addition to the expenses of the house, it was necessary to pay the children's school. We had to watch them. They had to be educated. He felt responsible for every act of the children and their future.

"No questions that children fail," he said to himself.

New stresses settled and were added to the previous ones. From now on, he no longer waited until his children reached the majority to be finally free. He had forgotten that his stopwatch was not stopped because he was getting older at the same time as his children were growing up. A majority of the children were retired. So on, until his seventy candles, he did not know why he had fought all this time. At all times, he yearned for something; but after he got it, he ended up bothering and rejecting it for other things. Now retired, he did not know what he had done about his life so far.

Time seemed to pass very quickly. By dint of capping in his house, stress won him. From time to time, he spent a little time at the neighbor's, also retired. They talked about everything because they had become true friends. They remembered their exploits, their love of youth. And above all, in a friendly way, they told each other humorous little anecdotes.

At their age, they felt isolated from the affairs of their families unless playing with the grandchildren who seemed to understand them. The times were over, and their stories seemed to be overwhelmed by their grown-up children.

One day, Komalo was with his neighbor in his house. They told each other their first love, and it was hilarity. It seemed that all their cheerfulness was hidden in their past. They understood each other, and they were aware of the unfinished nature of their childhood dreams. There was not much left to say unless they waited until the end because they had become old. Someone had just cut their laughter! He was dressed all in black, and his face was hidden in his hood, the look was down. Apparently, he was not familiar. The states were stopped. It was astonishment in the eyes of the unknown.

A few seconds passed without them articulating a word. They looked at the living room door and saw that it was closed. They tried to remember the movements announcing his arrival and felt themselves blocked by a sidereal silence. They exchanged questioning glances but could not find reasonable answers. Finally, Komalo managed to speak!

"Hey! Hey! What are you doing here? And how did you come in?"

The visitor remained without moving and without answering his questions.

They looked at each other again, surprised by this sordid presence. The atmosphere suddenly became icy cold. They were aware that something was wrong. They tried to stare at him, but the face of the stranger disappeared into his hood. They zoomed in to discern better but only glimpsed darkness. They tried to scrutinize him. And there, what they saw! The horror! He was not human! The fear overwhelmed them, and they clenched on the cushions of the sofas to escape this abomination. Thus, they protected their face, not to see it, but it remained engraved in their eyes, even closed. Terror paralyzed them, and they could neither move from their positions, nor emit any cry of relief.

With his mind and in a haphazard way, Komalo managed to talk to him. "Who are you?"

"The angel of death."

"What do you want from us?"

"I am not here today to look for you. However, I came to see your friend by announcing his last week of life."

"His last week of life!"

"We give him a chance to rebuild his life and make sense of it before it ends."

"What about me?"

"You have one month and ten days to live. I will come back for you. At forty days, your life cycle will be complete."

"One month, ten days! What do you mean?"

"Yes. It's up to you. There is no discussion. These durations were established even before you came to earth, and you had signed on your destiny books. This remains recorded in the big picture of destinies."

Before dissipating incognito, he repeated his words with a firm tone, "I'll come back. One thousandth of a second will not be allowed. One breath of air will not be granted."

They became normal again when the angel disappeared. Thus, they found their five senses again panting. Their hearts were pounding. They were scared, and they did not doubt what had happened.

One week for the one, and one month and ten days for the other, it seemed very insufficient in their eyes. They asked themselves questions without answers. Everyone summarized everything he had done since childhood but could not find anything conclusive to make sense of his life. According to the angel of death, they had spent their whole life until retirement without meaning. Yet, they thought they had lived properly. They had lived as their fathers and as the fathers of their fathers. They had lived like everyone else. And there, the angel confirmed them the opposite.

Komalo asked himself questions that could make sense of his life but found nothing but what he had chosen for life. It became a puzzle to find a solution. He looked at his friend, too, in the same disarray.

"How so my life does not make sense?" asked his friend.

Everyone with his concern.

Komalo did not even listen to him. He was sinking into the idea that he was going to die on the fortieth day from the moment. The neighbor who had only one week to live was not worried by the short duration, but rather by the lack of meaning to his life while he was retired. He tried to think but did not find a way to fix it. He felt himself lost without solution.

They remained there—sad, calm, and unanswered. In a short space of time, they were discouraged from any effort to fight for survival.

A few minutes earlier, they were in hilarity. Here, they were at the height of despair. Heads down, they did not talk anymore. How ephemeral life is! How ephemeral are these states of souls! Their lives were hanging by a thread. They would have liked not to know. They would have liked to be surprised by death. They preferred not to think about it during their lives. When someone spoke of anything revolving around death, they preferred not to listen to it. Otherwise, they changed the subject. It itched. It scared them. This unknown, yet known, was fled with great pace without getting rid of it. They did not suspect his inevitable existence. They knew it would happen, but they did not want to know the date. The deaths reminded them of his presence, but they did not want the look.

Despite their troubles, they felt lucky to be able to rebuild their lives, even though their time was very small in their eyes. At least the angel had warned them of the loss of meaning in their lives. They were now aware. Their respective stories ran through their heads. The regrets and remorse served as Stop signs and the success of green lights. They rode around for a few moments to discern what was wrong and what was on the rails.

A few moments later, they finally found the taste to talk about it.

"Now, what should I do?"

"I do not know. I ask myself the same question. What else do I have to do that I could not try?"

"We are badly blocked. Time is not enough to make something sensible. Look at us. What we have not been able to do until retirement, it is unthinkable to attempt it in such a short time."

"I think we can do something, even if the time allotted is ephemeral," Komalo told him.

"Like what?"

"I do not know, but if he asked us, it's because we're lucky to get there. This is the first time I see the angel of death coming to alert his prey. Besides, I've never heard it from anywhere."

"What are we going to do now?"

"Think about it and start working."

"I cannot even think. What will become of the house if I am no more? And the children? Well, they became adults. But my things, who will take care of it?"

He was asking all the questions that went through his mind. Everything he had built, or tried to build, came back to him. The already resolved cases posed a question of durability. Projects started and not yet completed also posed a management and monitoring problem. And finally, dreams not yet realized posed a problem of disappointment.

"I feel he's not kidding. He will come back for us."

"I do not think so. Anyway, I will not be able to do anything else that I have not tried to try."

"At least we try."

After a moment of reflection, he resumes.

"It is true that it would be wiser to ask him what to do," Komalo said.

\*\*\*\*\*

Six days later, Komalo's friend, seeing his countdown coming to a close and having realized nothing he had ever tried to do before, packed up his few belongings and wanted to leave the city for another destination before the angel of death returns. On the seventh day, he was out of breath in a remote area of another city. He curled up in a corner, where there was no human being, thinking he was escaping the angel.

Two minutes before the end of the expected time, he looked in all directions and saw no one coming from far away. He watched his watch without taking his eyes off him. The seconds passed by. There was only one minute, then thirty seconds, five seconds, four, three, two, and finally one second. The countdown was over! Thus, renewed hope crossed him. He relieved himself and relaxed, closing his eyelids slightly. A small smile of victory appeared on his lips.

Opening his eyelids, a surprise awaited him. The angel of death was in front!

"Did you think you were safe from death? You did not know that it is written in the big book of destinies that you were going to die today, at this place and at this time. You thought you were running away when you went to the right place. Your watch is two minutes ahead," the angel told him.

He took his life in excruciating pain. Despite the luck he had been given, he was not out of the routine because he was not prepared. Komalo, meanwhile, had taken this warning much more seriously. He took stock of his life, repented to all those he had met before bowing out.

*****

At the end of the anecdote, the great scholar turned to Makham's father and asked him a series of questions.

"And what would you do if you had one day to live? What would you do if you had a week to live to make sense of your life? What would you do if you had a month left to live to make sense of your life?"

At these onslaught of questions, Makham's father remained silent, with a meditative air. A moment later, inspired by the last moments of Komalo's life and repentance, he spoke again, "Repent and stay righteous for the rest of the time."

"So if we do not know the moment of its end, we must begin our repentance now."

Makham's father turned his head slightly toward the great scholar as a sign of enlightenment.

"I do not speak of you, for I know that your heart never stops talking about the Lord. You have in your hands the most precious that we expected, but you ignore it because it is hidden in its being by its seventy thousand luminous sails and as many dark sails."

At this moment, Makham returned to take refuge with his father who welcomed him with open arms. The great scholar resumed the rosary, grazing with a silent litany without paying any more attention to the crowd.

For minutes, no word was out of the scholar's mouth. However, people were getting impatient. His silence and his plunge into the litanies again gave rise to whispers.

A moment later, he asked the crowd to forgive him if he had offended anyone during his life. Voices from the crowd were quick to confirm that he had not offended anyone because, on the contrary, it was he who led them in the path of righteousness. He asked people to come forward if he had a forgotten debt to someone. These were the same answers from the crowd.

"You have no debts to anyone."

"Praise to God Lord of the universe," said the scholar.

People did not understand what had taken their great scholar to behave in this way. They had seen him greet the child fervently, then they had seen him curiously about this child before changing his speech. And finally, they had seen him asking for forgiveness as if he wanted to do his life check after telling an anecdote of impending death. Nobody knew what had happened between the child and the scholar. However, eyes scrutinized the child bluntly.

A moment later, the scholar became indisposed and left them. An enigmatic atmosphere followed without providing real answers.

A week later, as predicted by Makham, the great scholar died. These were great funerals. Anecdotes about his life were told by these admirers. He was considered a saint by his people. Some were quick to remember his last farewell meeting.

\*\*\*\*\*

The Sufi had left the continent where the star of knowledge of the heavenly chest was. He went to another continent in search of the third star. From country to country, he followed the wake of the astroid.

A few days later, he found himself in a street about ten meters from a sexagenarian who seemed to be unstable. He put his back to a post and seemed to ignore it.

When passersby approached, the individual stood up, shouting loudly, "Pray that God will not be first in your hearts." Then in a lower voice and sadness, he continued, "If so, there will be no room for anything else."

On these terms, people took heresy. Some passersby who knew him already did not fail to take the other way of the street to move away from him.

Half an hour passed without the Sufi approaching the individual. He was content to observe it momentarily. At a given moment, it was up to the individual to call him and talk to him.

"Come, ask your questions instead of putting yourself at that distance. Is not it that you come from far away for that? What are you waiting for?"

He approached with a smile on his lips.

"Ah! You knew I was there for you."

Here, everything is known.

"How did you know?"

"Your halo feels since you entered the city. And since then, I have been guiding you to me." He sat down beside him and listened to him finish his remarks. "Your quest is noble. And I can say that it is the most noble because it is about worrying about the good of humanity. Our prophet was sent only to be merciful to the worlds. And here you are, in his footsteps.

"With this awareness, why then do you say a prayer so that God is not first in people's hearts?"

"You have found the answer yourself. From the moment they decide to pray in this way, they believe in the existence of God, and this awareness was to prevent them from not doing it. Above all, do not forget the following, for the heart where God reigns cannot contain anything but him. He cannot be restrained neither, in the heavens, nor on the earth, but in the heart open to him."

"But this part you say it in a lower voice."

"This will allow people to ask questions about the words and to end up thinking about God, sometimes without realizing it."

"You are a big acquaintance."

"If you say so. However, only God knows."

Right then, he approached a baby in a stroller. His mother, who pushed him, seemed to ignore the individual who traumatized the passersby by his remarks. She took the adjacent lane.

At their height, the baby, excited, jumped in his stroller as if he wanted to leave. He struggled with all his might to reach the two individuals. Misunderstanding could be seen in her mother's attitude, for she had never seen him behave in this way, especially with strangers. She immediately tried to calm him down, but he persisted in going out.

Crying followed. The mother, a little embarrassed, tried to continue her way but an unexpected event happened. The baby was coming for the first time to shout "Dad."

His mother was surprised at this new behavior and ended up stopping. The two strangers got up and approached the baby. The tears turned into a laugh of joy. It was a small exchange of sign expressions between the baby and the two strangers. The mother flashed her eyes between this little world and found a certain harmony in their communication.

"How old is it?" asked the Sufi.

"Eight months two days," replied the mother.

So they started to discuss a little bit of everything from their favorite food to their berths. The person in charge of this unprecedented meeting seemed to be forgotten. Suddenly, he reminded them of his presence with cries.

"He confuses you with his father," said the mother.

"He's cute," said the star.

The baby gave him this remark of joy with laughter.

A moment later, after the baby's departure, the star spoke to the Sufi. "Babies know how to see."

"Hum!"

"They only see reality, but growing the mysteries of this world end up veiling their eyes."

A moment of silence, then the star spoke again, "The goal is God. His path is righteousness while the lantern is knowledge. The best mount is faith. The engine is love while its fuel is hope. It is enough to accelerate by fervor to get there in time." He paused before continuing, "Is it as easy or difficult as that?"

"You are really a scholar."

"Since you insist on me, I will tell you, in an imaginative way, the story of Solomon and the fish of God. It must be taken as parabolic. Okay?"

The Sufi was already used to parabolic tales since, since the beginning of his quest, he was only following the signs and interpreting the parables to detect the hidden side of things.

# Solomon and the Fish of the Divine

The world had certainly known kings, sometimes even great kings, but none of them had equaled Solomon. Some kings had managed to become emperors. They had succeeded in uniting tribes from three continents. They commanded large armies of men. They had erected great temples and monuments. Nevertheless, none of them had equaled by his power, by his organizational character, by the number of his subjects, and by the extent of his territories, that of Solomon. He was not only king of the earth's human beings but also king of spirits and animals. He was the king of all living things on earth, human beings, animals, and jinns. His power was such that the whole earth was under his command. On earth, his power was as widespread in the visible world as in the intelligible world. He was often informed of what was going on in the distant lands of his kingdom by birds and jinns. Each species was so well-organized as a military organization. The species were grouped around a species commander and formed a genus. The genres were organized with a commanding kind to form a family. Families formed a region. Each region presented three commanders, that of the animals, that of the human beings, and finally that of the jinns. So all his kingdom was so well structured that none of these beings had ever seen such a similar.

Solomon was overwhelmed by the grace of his lord. All he needed was he got it without much effort. His innumerable subjects were at his services day and night. All beneficence of this land was for him at hand. If the service was urgent, the jinn jostled for the privilege of doing the act. Each with his techniques to accomplish the mission as quickly as possible. For them, it was a great honor to have a mission from his majesty. Daily reports were not lacking. As a result, Solomon was aware of all that was happening in his kingdom, the land—both in animals, humans, and Djinns. He ruled unchallenged. He was able to solve all his problems, which proved extremely rare.

One day, to thank his lord who had showered him with blessings still unmatched on earth, Solomon asked him to assist him in his work.

"Oh my god, lord of the universe, you have filled me to be king of the earth. I do not miss anything. I would like to thank you. Thank you."

God accepted his thanks, but Solomon did not stop there. He continued, "Now let me help you feed all your creatures so that you can rest during this time.

"You cannot," replied God.

"So let me help you feed them for a year."

At this moment, Solomon thought he had apprehended everything with the power his lord had bestowed upon him, for he was the king of the earth.

In spite of his deep love for him and his enthusiasm, God repeated the same answer to him.

"You cannot."

Amazed, Solomon looked to the east and saw an infinity of his subjects waiting for his order. The crowd disappeared into the horizon. At the same moment, a strident houa came from the crowd to show his determination. All imaginable tools were brandished. There were agricultural tools and kitchen utensils. They were ready.

Solomon turned to the west, and it was the same scenery he saw. An interminable crowd stood before him. Another sign of presence and determination was emitted by the crowd. He looked north, it was the same thing. Animals intertwined with humans and spirits. It was the same south. The whole earth listened only to its starting signal. He found himself surrounded by a crowd whose boundaries disappeared in the horizon, in the four cardinal points.

A great houa, coming from all over, was breaking down to Solomon, and this galvanized him. So he turned to God and spoke to him again.

"So let me feed them for a month."

It was always the negation on the part of God.

"You cannot."

Solomon turned to his innumerable subjects and was astonished at the denial of God. He spoke again, addressing God with a voice of astonishment this time.

"For a week!"

And it was always the negation on the part of God.

He was not discouraged thereby to make this sign of thanks to his lord. He continued, "If I cannot feed them for a week, so let me feed them for a day."

God did not change his mind.

"You cannot."

So Solomon wondered again.

"Yet I am the king of the earth, the king of animals, king of humans and spirits!"

He tried to count his numbers and found that it covered the whole earth. He tried to probe their devotion and found that they were ready to die and rot for him. He tried to evaluate their cumulative forces and found that they could lift mountains. However, he persisted in wanting to feed all the creatures of God.

Solomon turned to God again. "Lord, I asked you to let me feed all your creatures. You told me that I will not be able. I asked you for a year. It's the same, for a month. You answered the same thing. For a week, it's the same. Also, there is no change of opinion for a day. Now please let me feed them for a meal."

Faced with Solomon's stubbornness to do good for his lord and his insistent prayer, God obeyed and gave him permission to try.

"You can try."

It was a cry of victory from the crowd. They had had the agreement, coming from their king, to start the preparation of the dishes.

"From today and for a month, only work for food preparation," Solomon addressed his people.

The stopwatch was triggered and activities began. For a month, Solomon's empire cooked and gathered food. The expected time was coming to an end. The days disappeared. The hours passed. There were no more minutes. He stayed five seconds, four seconds, three seconds, two seconds, one second. Suddenly, everything faded. They had respected their king so much that they had respected the rendezvous to the nearest second. It had been a month dead.

Solomon defiled before the dishes and was satisfied with the work of his people. He was smiling. Thus, 120 rays of food, each of which was three kilometers in length, were formed. He had not skimped on the means. There were all kinds of food, from everyday foods to the most complex foods to be prepared.

Solomon proudly turned to God and spoke to him, "Now you can send your creatures—"

Before even finishing his speech, a huge fish came out of the ocean, swallowed all at once with his tongue all the dishes that had taken a month to prepare. It was a total astonishment. Mouth open, the people had never imagined the existence of such a creature. The fish soon swallowed his meal. However, all thoughts were directed toward other creatures that had not yet arrived.

Without speaking to him, he turned to Solomon, removing with his tongue pieces of tablets embedded in his teeth.

"What are you waiting for?" the fish told him.

*What!* Solomon wondered.

Opening the eyes wide, as a sign of astonishment, the fish continued, "There remain the other two-thirds! God sent me to you. He told me that you want to insure my meal today. You gave me the third, so I have the other two-thirds left. It's you I'm waiting for."

There, Solomon knew he was badly barred. He had nothing else to offer to his new assignment. He had spent a month gathering food, thinking it could feed all of God's creatures. So that it was enough for a single individual to take away a whole month's labor, which was not satisfactory.

Being stubborn in front of God, he was forever embarrassed. He searched for solutions but could not find any, while his worry of being overwhelmed by other creatures grew. He was now aware not only of the little knowledge God had given him in comparison with divine knowledge, but also of the tiny power he held despite his privilege as king of the earth.

So he turned to God with a humble voice. "Lord, allow me to repent of this obstinacy. You are really the savant, the lord of the all power."

*****

Thus, the star turned toward the Sufi while continuing his narration. "God has created creatures that ignore the very existence of the human being. Tell yourself that all knowledge is relative, except that which he knows himself. He is his brilliant light that extends over all existence and encompasses it in all its places. There are seventy-seven existential dimensions of the divine word in the visible and in the invisible. It only takes one misinterpretation from a great disciple to deceive an entire people for generations, even millennia.

"Sometimes, these disciples interpret well, but, at very high levels, what is very rarely achieved by the common people, and it easily induces to deviate from reality.

"Every cause has a consequence, and every consequence has a cause. Afflictions, debases, and so many other unpleasant things are not always what we think. As long as you think you are believing, expect to be tested. He is the only Savant, the Master of the all-powerful."

A moment of silence, then he continued, "If you give him your goods, he will fructify them and preserve them here. If you give him your soul, he will lift it up to its proximity. And if you give him your goods and your soul, you will remain in the eternal enjoyment.

*****

At the end of his narration, the illuminated man turned again to the Sufi before asking him a question that turned out to be the same as that posed by the previous star.

"What did you understand?"

"God is the Savant. He is at the origin of the most accurate knowledge. He is also the Lord of the Omnipotence."

"And?"

74

"He created creatures that ignore the existence of the human being. He has also created creatures unknown to man.

"Yes."

A moment later, he took an old ring out of his pocket and handed it to the Sufi. "I do not have much to offer you to accompany you on your quest. I only have that."

He scrutinized it for a long time. Ideas crossed his head. *It's a ring pattern that you do not see all the time! It looks like an antique ring!*

The illuminated man cut his dreams as if he heard the intimacy that was visible in the Sufi's head. "It's an old-fashioned model, but it belongs to you now. You can do whatever you want. Perhaps, it will be useful to you at the opportune moment." He ended his remarks with a big, enigmatic smile.

"God only knows. He is the source of truth."

The Sufi thanked him for his benevolence, without giving too much importance to his gift. They greeted each other and left each other with hearts full of joy.

After the departure of the illuminated, the Sufi scrutinized the ring again but did not find it important. Thus, the words of the illuminated returned to him in the head: *It's an old-fashioned model, but it belongs to you now. You can do whatever you want...*

Without thinking, he threw the ring near a trash can before continuing his way.

\*\*\*\*\*

Two days passed. A garbage collector who was picking up garbage cans saw the ring. He took it and scrutinized it for a long time but found it of no use, as the Sufi did.

\*\*\*\*\*

75

Days passed, and the people who saw it ended up throwing it again because in front of their eyes, nobody would want such an old and ugly ring.

*****

A week passed, then the Sufi, during a walk, wanted to afford before leaving the city and passed the same place. A few feet away, he saw a passerby pick up the ring, scrutinized it, and threw it before continuing on.

The Sufi approached and saw the ring on the floor. He hesitated to pick it up. However, the goodness and clairvoyance of the enlightened came back to him as a souvenir. Finally, he leaned over and picked up the ring. He tried to insert it into his finger, but it was too big for everyone, even for the thumb. He did not know what to do with it, despite his thought in memory of the illuminated. He hesitated to throw it again. Then, in a burst of jet, raising slightly his head a little further, he saw a cotton thread. Immediately, an idea crossed his mind. He picked up the thread, passed it through the ring, and put it around his neck.

Some time later, he was in his hotel, packing his bags to take the plane that was to leave three hours later.

# The Ups and Downs of Life

A taxi picked him up at the hotel for the airport. Time passed because traffic jams kept him in the traffic. Momentarily, he froze on his watch to count the minutes he had left before the plane took off. Unable to leave the vehicle with his suitcases, nor able to abandon them to walk, he was contented to count the seconds that continued to flow toward the time of the appointment. The traffic jam was long, and the vehicles moved just a few meters to stop again. The time passed.

When the taxi finally arrived at the airport, the plane had already left. The ticket, which was not refundable, ended up being lost. The next plane going in the same direction will be leaving the next day, so he turned back to the hotel. To mitigate his pain, he offered himself a bottle of yoghurt before going back in a taxi. The traffic jams were not over, and the return to the hotel became as dangerous as the way out.

In full circulation, his belly was heard. Bloating followed. He looked at the expiration date and saw that it had expired for several months. The rectum could no longer hold all its gaseous assaults; he rushed to leave the vehicle in full traffic. He looked for the nearest place to relieve this unexpected need, but the one spotted seemed far away. He ran, like a person before death, to preserve his dignity. He entered a house without permission. He met a tenant who was running away from him as an abuser. He tried to temper the atmosphere but what was swarming in his belly was stronger. He asked for the toilet, but the resident was slow to answer him. He gestured in sign language but was not understood. He searched the premises without even asking permission and finally found the WC.

At his forced entry into the toilet, the tenant eventually understand his imminent need to relieve himself. At this moment, the traffic became fluid, and the horns of the other vehicles from behind forced the taximan to advance. He looked for a place to park, but all the spaces were busy. In his quest for parking, he was moving away. At the first crossing, he tried to go around the lot to pick up his client but was held back in a traffic jam.

When he left the toilet, the Sufi did not delay asking the tenant for forgiveness. The latter accepted the apology and advised him to take all his time to ensure he could return without genes.

A moment later, he left the house but did not find the taxi. He stood there, waiting for more than an hour without his luggage, while all his money and papers were inside. He had not picked up the taxi number, nor did he know how to find a taxi driver he could not even recognize if he pictured himself. He finally concluded that this baggage was lost.

In front of this brackish destiny, he did not know what to do. The hours passed, and the bodily needs demanded satisfaction. He left the neighborhood to roam the streets, hoping to find solutions to his situation. The unthinkable was invading him. He had never thought of finding himself without any money, paper, or home in another continent different from his own. His dismay was great because he knew that his country of origin did not have an embassy or consulate in this country.

A moment later, the taxi driver, in good faith, returned to the same place, but the Sufi was already gone. He did not know where to look for it. He finally left the luggage in the house, hoping that one day, the Sufi would go back to look for them. It was the beginning of a sinister gear in the corridor of his quest.

The more hours passed, the more critical his situation became. He stayed for three days in the street without eating. In this respect, his physical strength dwindled. Arrived at the corner of a street, he snuggled to the ground to appease his hunger. Some people who believed him beggar came to throw him some coins. He raised his head and saw the money he could not refuse despite his meager market value. He left it on the ground without paying too much attention.

Moments later, other people were throwing in again. The more time passed, the more his recipes increased. He ended up picking them up and went to buy a sandwich. He ate it greedily. And it was his first meal for several days. However, the sandwich did not seem to satisfy him.

Having no other source of revenue, he immediately returned to the corner of the street to snuggle as before. So, unwittingly, he was begging to survive.

The days passed, and his social debasement became evident. His only coat he wore since was colorful with the colors of dirt. Hunger, hypothermia, insomnia, and loneliness overwhelmed him. Faced with his helplessness in the face of this fate, he no longer hesitated to beg. To increase his income, he momentarily changed his place in order to find himself in front of passersby. He had become unrecognizable. His hair was full of curls. His clothes were torn apart and began to be ragged.

One day, sitting on the floor as usual, he tried to trace the origin of his shrinkage but found no reason. Suddenly, the words of the onirocritic scholar he had consulted came back to him. *Know that the one who has fully realized the station of absolute servitude is exposed to the test.* He immediately concluded that his depreciation was linked to his quest. He tried to find solutions to get out but found none.

A moment later, he lost himself again in the world of dreams, and other words of the scholar came back to him. *If one does not have deep faith, one will never go far because what is veiled by the mystery of the celestial vault transcends the eyes of the common man. You will need faith. This is the only mount to overcome the obstacles strewn on the path. Thus, a smile appeared at the end of his lips as an understanding.*

Hours passed, and his heart accepted all the unpleasant events he was undergoing. All his attachments to life and his turpitude were dissipated. No longer seeking to leave the continent, he was content to survive. He sometimes asked for leftovers from the shopkeepers along a large street in the city. His big compassionate smile attracted the sympathy of the people. Little by little, they recognized it, and it was part of the city's decor. His country was far away, but he considered himself a resident of the city as if he had always been there.

One day, while begging from shop to shop, he went to the antique dealer who handed him a coin. Before leaving the shop, something caught the eyes of the septuagenarian on the beggar's chest. He invited her to return to him, which the beggar did, without delay. The antiquarian held out his hand and took out the ring which was hidden under the beggar's clothes. It was astonishment. He did not believe his eyes. The atmosphere became calm again immediately.

"Wait, I'll double-check. Certainly, it's a perfect copy," said the antiquary.

After a few minutes of minute observation under the indifferent eyes of the beggar, the antiquary uttered a eureka. It was an apotheosis that the beggar did not understand.

"Where did you find this relic?" asked the antiquarian.

"I was given it as a gift."

"Do you know what it is?"

"Yes. It's a ring."

"No. I wanted to say, what is its value?"

He remained meditative, then the words of him who had given it to him came back to him.

Without delay, he answered him in the same way. "God only knows."

"It's an inestimable ring. This is the ring of the prophet Solomon."

"Hum! What do you mean?"

"It's a ring that was a bonus of a lot of money. With this money, you can become very rich."

He immediately remembered the indifference he accorded and accorded by passersby to this jewel, which was invaluable.

With the consent of the beggar, the antiquary soon called the national museum of the country. A specialized team was dispatched on site. After verification by the specialists, they confirmed the authenticity of the relic. The beggar was immediately given a lot of importance because he would become very rich. The country's authorities paid him his money in an account and then gave him a nationality with papers to travel around the world.

*****

A few days later, his face changed. In a five-star hotel, in front of buffets of several different dishes, he shook his head in surprise before monologizing.

"God only knows. Look, how I was during his two years in the street, with all the tortures of life, while I wore around my neck an inestimable value!"

*****

A month later, the signs of a rich person were not long in seeing each other. He bought himself a house and a vehicle. Unable to drive, he offered the service of a driver.

One day, he visited the antique dealer, who was delighted to see him again in his new clothes.

"I came for two things. One, to see you again and thank you for your assistance, and two, to buy something back in the shop. I know I will not be able to buy everything. And if that were the case, I would not know what to do with it. Maybe other people will need it. What am I going to do, offer me the oldest item in the shop that cannot be sold," said the Sufi, the ex-beggar.

"If that is your will, I will only bow to it. In this case, I have to search the depot."

The antiquary entered the other room and took out an old and twisted horn of an unknown animal. "This is the oldest bit in the shop. I have acquired it since the opening of the shop, forty years ago now. I remember like it was yesterday, but nobody wanted it. People prefer what is infatuated with history. The more the story or the characters who acquired it are famous, the more valuable the object is. Most say that the horns are not bought, just go to the slaughterhouse to find free galore."

"Give me a price," said the Sufi.

"It does not have much market value. That's why I cannot sell it."

"What does it matter that people value it? I give it value."

"And what will you do with it?"

"To expose it in my house, and every time I see it again, this will bring me to remember that life is ephemeral. We can die overnight. And for me, this state of consciousness is priceless."

After a brief hesitation and at the insistence of the Sufi, he finally articulated, "I cannot ask you anything for that. Give what you want."

"It's the same thing I said to myself about the ring, and you took me out of this ignorance. So I'll give you half of the money in exchange for the horn."

Eyes wide open, the antique dealer did not believe it. The Sufi made him a check while thanking him warmly.

When he arrived home, he exposed the horn in the living room, and this contrasted with the modern environment. He paid much attention to the horn not because of its market value but rather because of his reminder of the life experience he had experienced in the city. From a simple traveler, he was compelled to remain, with the loss of all his property, to extreme poverty. Then, with a stroke of grace, he became socially important in this country. However, he had not forgotten his quest. He had to find the fourth star that was to be in another continent. It was a great preparation as this will complete his guidance to find the keeper of the key to the safe.

From the beginning of his quest, he had traveled to distant lands to meet great unsuspected mystics. With this great ambition, life had not spared him from his many stigmas. However, he did not shudder because guided by knowledge on the mount of faith.

*****

The earth turned, and months had passed. The Sufi found himself in another continent. He walked in a very narrow alley. Passersby had to put their backs against the wall to let those coming in the opposite direction to pass. He passed a few individuals, and then his arm brushed against a guy. They seemed to project into another universe. The two looks were unearthed and then followed sketches of smile. Before the Sufi uttered a word, the passerby challenged him with an invitation.

"Do not forget me in your quest."

"How did you know?"

"I heard your soul-searching for me in the city, and then I came to meet you."

"I come from the neighboring continent."

"I know."

"How?"

At this moment, the other passersby of the two senses became impatient.

"What we will do, I will invite you to take coffee. Let's go to let others."

They took different narrow streets of a large slum. They sat on two stools in front of a small cart. The order was launched, and a few moments later, two steaming cups were served. They sipped their liquid in a family atmosphere. The Sufi guest in his fifties was dressed soberly, with a shirt and trousers. It was up to the native to speak again.

"So did you want some supra-luminous guidance?"

"I have to go to this treasure."

"For that, you will need perfection."

"Perfection?"

"Yes, perfection. This rare pearl."

"A pearl!"

"It's the sparkling diamond of excellence. He is poured indefinitely into the truth."

The discussion was interrupted by the occupant of the cart, which served them cakes.

"Many are men who aspire to rise and who ignore this state of mind. I'll tell you an anecdote about a facet of this perfection."

The Sufi, with the meeting of the three previous stars of wisdom, used to listen to these fabulous parables infused with immense wisdom. He had learned a lot during his various journeys, but despite all, these scholars advised him *to go to the quest for knowledge.*

Breath mastered, mind freed, eyes in the interstices of the universe, he began to narrate under the attentive listening of the Sufi.

# Perfection

Everywhere on earth, prayers were sounding, day and night. Those who aspired to spirituality wanted to access perfection. May divinity descend into them. This pearl was for those who had only light in their hearts. However, tirelessly, without resignation, always on time, loudly and quietly, people kept looking for it because it was the ultimate access: perfection.

The race was launched, and the pearl was there. The first one able to access it perhaps deserves this jewel. The most sublime treasure! To be perfect was to be in permanent communion with the source of the deity who is the perfect.

The crowd was huge, and the desire was felt everywhere. In the sky appeared the jewel on a charitable crown, and wearing it provided tranquility. Seventy thousand angels carried it on every meaning. The majestic descent showed impatience in the crowd.

Ten thousand hordes were unleashed. Thus, the scramble had begun, and the competition was declared. Everyone claimed to be the worthiest to receive him. Each individual displayed his beneficence, and his own praise was soon heard. The family trees were drawn, and the exploits listed. The numbers of supporters were encrypted, and the ways of dressing unveiled. The most beautiful places of worship were brandished. Higher and bigger it was, the better it was convincing.

From time to time, punches were exchanged. The fight was unleashed. Blood gushed. Clothes were torn. People were confused. Injuries were as far as the eye could see, and in the four cardinal directions. The nearest, physically, was the first to declare war. The overriding objectives were lost in the wake. Some stood against each other, and lives were falling.

The pearl was within reach for those who had been allowed to gather. But by dint of fighting to seize it, the hearts hardened, whereas this jewel could only merge with a receptacle of the divine mercy.

A five-year-old child used to draw figures on the floor. When he was alone, his hobby was drawing what came into his head on the fine sand of his village. Sometimes, it was geometric figures; sometimes creatures out of the ordinary. He did not know the meaning of all these drawings, but he was familiar with this mysterious world. One had the impression that he was in osmosis with formulas and signs not running, which gave him peace of mind.

From time to time, unknown words of common language crossed his head. He was innocent. He was only a child of five, and he did not know the world of adults and its limits. For him, everything seemed normal. His perception of the world was normal perception as he was treading an unknown world even for most adults.

Sitting on a dune, his eyes crossed the worlds. He played to go to scenes in different worlds, like a person in front of his TV in 4D. It was like the tales and fables that were often told to him by his grandfather.

In the modern world, this would look like phantasmagorical movies banned to at least sixteen years old. It was not uncommon to see him sit on the ground with his legs bent, his head on his knees, his fists on his cheeks, and be captivated in these extraordinary worlds. He used to redraw on the ground the images he remembered in those worlds. Among these images and figures, some had been lost and erased in the memory of all the adults of these worlds because of their quarrels of yesteryear. Henceforth, these symbols were known only to angelic spirits, except him. Perhaps it was because of his young age and his innocence that the angels had let him drag his images and formulas into his mind. He was innocent of the ravings of his mind. He was oblivious to the content of his visions. On land, some were willing to give everything they had and everything they could have to take his place.

Out of unconsciousness, he had spotted all his clothes and toys with the ultimate symbol. The latter was drawn on the supreme chest and testifying to its presence in the sealed enclosure.

He was playing with these symbols while this was important. He was unaware of his love with these signs. His parents either did not know why he was passionate about unusual drawings and figures. Sometimes, he showed them some drawings that they always appreciated to avoid evicting him from his universe. They admired him. They pampered him and found him a gift and intellectual maturity, but still, they considered him a child. It was evident! It was their child.

One day, still on the dune, he had walked the unknown. In addition to drawing the ultimate symbol on the floor, a word was uttered by his heart unconsciously. It was the door of presence!

Suddenly, he was sucked into a kind of luminous vortex and found himself in another dimension. All his senses were activated at their height. He saw, smelled, and heard in four dimensions. He found himself at the center of a din. The number of presents seemed to be infinite. Everyone was waiting, eyes riveted up, the descent of the celestial crown.

Halfway, the crowd was unleashed. The scramble became a universal brawl. Everyone wanted to be crowned with this jewel, perfection. Old men were no longer recognized as fellows. The weapons were taken out of their sheaths, and all sorts of weapons were brandished, each with what it hid in its bowels. Corpses were trampled, and the fight ensconced in cascade.

The child tried to make his way not to access this jewel, but rather to avoid beating his adults, like a child in a battle. He stepped over corpses. He avoided walking on the wounded and tried to assist the mutilated. He soon took three dates out of his pocket and gave it to the wounded.

Arrived in a corner, he stood behind a window to understand what was happening in this world. What he had seen horrified him. Tolerance, dignity, and hospitality were gone. The material had become the owner of humans despite their knowledge, despite their consciences, and despite their stories. He came out and found himself again in the heart of the unleashed crowd. His questions about the origin of these fights had no answers. The angels in tight ranks were still motionless, indifferent to this desolation. Their goal was to bring this sparkling diamond to the worthiest person to be crowned. The genetic origins, the exploits, the fortunes, the colors of the skin, and the numbers of partisans were transformed into heavy burdens for those who wore them. The child did not know who to speak to.

A moment of observation, he lives in the crowd of lonely people, who apparently were not involved in his fights and arguments. He immediately headed straight for them, but at each approach, it was disappointment. The person took advantage of his approach to rush to another to shoot him down. Desolation was on his face because he did not understand anymore. The image was only second nature.

A moment later, he dodged blows from everywhere, but his small size allowed him to sneak between the belligerents. He saw from afar in the crowd, between the different enemies, an old man with a curvilinear back leaning on a cane. He watched her for a moment and saw that he did not participate in the conflicts. Hope returned to him, and the features of his face became luminous again.

Baldness and canitia had invaded the head of the seemingly centenary old man. His long white beard was almost touching the ground. It was barely standing, leaning on a cane slightly above it. His arched body showed stigmas of a centennial to 1,001 lives. His physical strength seemed to have abandoned him for a long time.

The old man straightened up and stumbled on his feet. Momentarily, he remained motionless to breathe and recover his strength, still both hands resting on his cane. After a long, hesitant observation, the child finally made his way to the old man, hoping internally for comfort. He reminded him of his grandfather and the affection he gave him. Thus, the beating of his heart became soothed again. He was finally thinking he had found someone who could answer him on the reason of these rifts and which country they were in. He took the risk of fiddling again with his fists, his axes, his clubs, and all sorts of weapons.

Arrived at the old man, before even speaking to him, he was taken as a target by the latter. The blow of the cane brushed his hair. Thus, he rushed to give explanations, but it gave the appearance of not understanding the young boy. The clumsiness of his blows allowed the child to avoid him. However, the boy did not give up his invitations to peace with his arguments.

The old man whirled around his cane to face the boy, as the boy followed his spinning motion behind him to avoid confrontation. The old man got tired because he was not used to spending so much effort. He breathed very loud, mouth wide open. Nevertheless, he wanted to engage in the battle like everyone else.

Finally, the boy managed to articulate well in front of the old man.

"Grandfather, why this great battle between congeners?"

In a bruised and tired voice, the old man answered him, panting, "I do not know. I am the eldest of all, but they do not want me to beat them. I too do not let anyone access it before me."

"What is the jewel?"

"It's the Pearl of Perfection."

With a conscience and intellect in paroxysm, the boy continued the dialogue. "But! It is intended only for peaceful people! Why are you fighting then?"

"They are not more deserving than me. Look at me. I do not have any teeth anymore. I am over a hundred years old, and I have spent all my life praying to be part of this gathering."

"For this reason, keep your starting principles. If you are selected here, it is because you had something good that you cultivate. Do not get dragged into this squabble. Do not spoil your whole life with divine quest and piety.

"You are still young, my boy. You must be the age of my great-grandson. You do not know anything about life, especially if you have witnessed the disappearance of all those who were close and loved.

The old man's voice immediately became sad. Probably his memory reminded him, a nostalgia, of people who were dear to him.

With a quick gesture as if alerted by something, he turned his head toward the boy, asking him a question, "And you, why all these questions? Are not you here for the pearl?"

"Of course I was selected for this gathering, but not for war to be perfect. On the contrary, I try to be at peace with myself, and any benefit will be welcome.

"Why are you here then? If you do not fight, they will fight you."

In a higher voice, the old man spoke jerkily, "Go. Get away from me, or I'll crush you."

Seeing this old man wanting to fight and who could not even stand up properly, the young boy went desolate, shaking his head. He did not understand what was going on around him. Thus, he went away backing away, tears in his eyes.

\*\*\*\*\*

A strong Herculean man had just defeated his opponent. He walked toward the jewel. The old man was four meters away from him. He ignored him. He passed him slightly, giving him a piercing and threatening look, but the old man adopted an air of submission. Thus, the strong man went on leaving his back. It seemed he under-estimated him because of his advanced age. The old centenarian man seemed to be annoyed by this contemptuous attitude.

From behind, with his cane pointed end, he pierced the heart of the strong. It collapsed immediately. Both knees on the floor. He turned his head slightly and saw the terrifying old man.

"It's only an old man who is burying me!" the strong man murmured.

At these words, he ended up falling flat on his stomach.

Everything was sad. They tore each other apart. They killed each other. Bodies lay everywhere. Yet they had aspired so much for perfection, but their attachment to titles, material, and fame had diverted them from utility. He did not stop at the sturdy one; from time to time, on the lookout, like everyone else, the old man gave deadly blows to all those who tried to get ahead of him, most of whom did not know him because of his advanced age.

\*\*\*\*\*

Some had managed to get close to the pearl after so many fights and so many victories. However, the angels did not intervene despite the cruel wounds of some blood-stained individuals. Others had ragged clothes and private parties exhibited because of the battles they had fought.

They remained indifferent. By all the senses, there were seventy thousand standing guard and in rank tight around the crown, like beams of light emanating from a sphere. They seemed to be in communion with the heart of the crown, like a shining star of a thousand fires. It was up to the pearl to tell them what to do. They were only waiting for his order to act. Moreover, they were only created for his service.

*****

A man, in his fifties, was within reach of the pearl, which appeared in the form of a sphere the size of a soccer ball. Immediately, his size grew bigger. The man could not catch it in his hands since its progressive diameter had reached ten meters. He looked for formulas of incantations. His tongue stirred, but his heart was unable to react. He said to himself, "Still, I knew the formula!"

It was the password to participate in this rally. He tried to remember his acceptance to participate in the selection. The memories came back vaguely. He remembered being in meditation in a spiritual retreat that had lasted six months. He did not leave his room unless he went to the bathroom. To avoid meeting people, he had built toilets adjoining his room. Even his four wives were not allowed to see him in this isolation. The food was left in front of the door, and he slipped his hand out of the curtain to get them into the room. For him, this allowed him to avoid the temptation before any charm. He was fasting most of the time and spending all his time praying. He practically deprived himself of all bodily pleasures. His weight had dropped by half, and his sleep was reduced to two hours a night. For thirty-three years, every year, twice, three months of withdrawal were made in order to be selected to be part of this gathering.

At his thirty-third year in a row, he ended up receiving what he was looking for. A code of access to the chosen group, symbolizing the last name, was blown into his mind. This same secret code allowed to open the lock of perfection. It was enough to pronounce it before her to open and cover the person concerned. He spent most of his time repeating the code so he would not forget it, but there his memory seemed to betray him. He tried to concentrate in his being but still he did not remember anything. All his efforts, which were read on his actions, proved futile.

At this moment, the sphere was growing larger. It was around ten meters in diameter. In contact with this titanic luminous ball, his hands began to burn. He knew now that he was not the lucky winner crowned with the pearl. Fright and despair were invading him. He wondered why he was rejected and did not find an answer. Yet he had been chosen for this gathering after so many years of prayer, meditation, aspiration to divinity, not to say, total devotion.

With an abrupt and elastic movement, the incandescent sphere projected him far into the center of the unbridled crowd, where he fell on two belligerents by splashing them. He did not rise from his wounds. His guts had intertwined with the sand. However, the sphere returned to its size and initial brightness. She slipped slowly between the brawlers, but they did not pay attention because they were occupied by their opponents.

The sphere was always surrounded by angels who followed it in its movement. As she grew up, they grew up at the same time as marks on an inflatable balloon. Its light glittered with all the visible and invisible colors. Its translucent nature was lighter than rock water. Its density was more important than a black hole, and its weight heavier than the universe. Nobody could use it unless they had intrinsic virtues.

*****

A group of people had just seen the sphere rolling slowly not far from them. The sphere stabilized again in the middle of the crowd. The battle intensified. It was the frantic race. At each attempt to capture the sphere, it behaved the same as the firstcomer. In less than a thousandth of a second, it inflated to a diameter of ten meters before retracting to return to its original size. Those who tried to stop him were crushed by his weight. Those who sought to touch him were roasted to the core by his titanic heat. And finally, those who sought to penetrate it were propelled very far by its elasticity.

Fighting people had forgotten the password. They were immediately rejected from a distance by perfection. People were decimated as he passed. They could not take advantage of its proximity. However, from attempts to attempts, the sphere was moving slowly, rolling toward another group of individuals. The sphere seemed to despise the crowd that was previously selected. The most deserving of them was to be the one elected, but they were all the same.

Who could be elected in this general squabble since it had passed old and old, people with royal coats, and those in frocks, bearded, and mustachios, big and small, costaux and puny?

The sphere had left piles of corpses in its wake. Despite this damage, the quarrels continued. It was common to see the sphere move from one place to another. In a view of the sky, his wake described the figure of the secret code, but nobody could notice it because they were all in the same system—that of the mundane, that of their father and the father of their father. They were in their own system and were not trying to get out of it to understand it better. The boy remained motionless. He did not know where to go.

At 360 degrees, the decor was the same. The sphere was now heading toward the direction of the boy. She slipped slowly between their feet. She feigned the individuals trying to stop him. Sometimes, she shrank to the size of a billiard ball; sometimes it was the size of a football. A higher consciousness seemed to animate him. She seemed drawn to a force toward the boy. The child turned his head slightly to the right, here it is at hand. The boy hesitated to touch it.

Time seemed to flow to infinity. He closed his eyes and asked himself questions. *What is the point of having something that is at the root of all wars?* A feeling of astonishment arises from his heart. *Now those people on earth who were considered the wisest would tear each other apart!* A certainty crossed his head. *They are really ignorant!*

In his dreams, without even taking the initiative to take possession of it like his fellow creatures, the sphere ended by touching him. His heart beat to the rhythm of secrecy as the sphere began to spread its light into the boy's hand. He had not pronounced the code of the box but gradually, the sphere diminished in size as if transfused in the body of the boy. Suddenly, all movement faded on this world. The whole nature froze on this event. The stars stared at him by their radiance. The galactic forces were annihilated. The whole universe was only beating in one rhythm, in unison.

At half volume, the sphere and its heart were one. Immediately, the angels looked around him. He then saw his infinite power. From now on, they were only at his command. In his being, he felt a new infinite power. He knew he did not have to defend himself against anything anymore. The guardian angels would crush any imprudent one. He had not fought to grab it, but he had been chosen. And that was what most did not know.

A voice murmured in his being, *Perfection is not won by war, rather it is created by the serenity of the heart.*

With this power, the boy projected himself in time and saw how people would be rolled, some imprudently, others by the evil that rages in them. Immediately, with a sudden movement, he withdrew his hand. Thus, the light went back into the sphere. Everything became as before, and the boy faced the sphere surrounded by angels. He was afraid of himself and of what he was capable of.

Time passed without the boy making a decision. What he had just seen had traumatized him. He turned his head on all sides and saw that the antagonists had not yet stopped their fighting despite a short break. He was aware that he would not be spared in this squabble, even though he could be the holder of the crown of perfection. He was aware that at that moment, even if he did not really want it, he would crush any abuse as the sphere had just shown him. Fear and desolation intermingled with despair. He was also aware that as long as the sphere was not taken, the fighting would continue in this universe.

On earth, he could never believe what he had just lived. The people who were involved in this perdition were among the most aspiring to divinity. It is up to the sphere to address him in his heart by telepathy.

"*What are you waiting for?*"

"*I wonder about the consequences of your power in me.*"

"*That's what you just saw. You are the worthiest person present here to receive me.*"

"*Me, it is not to smite the people that I came. It is rather to taste the fruit of perfection.*"

"*I know. And I know what you do not know.*"

"*I prefer not to receive you and be imperfect to possess you and destroy others.*"

At once, the sphere changed color. His envelope became denser in this regard before continuing, "*That's what makes you different from others. My light cannot be contained in the heavens, or on the earth, but it can be contained in a merciful heart. Here, you are shown the virtues of perfection.*"

At this moment, the pearl engulfed the young boy. It narrowed and disappeared into his body. It went straight to his heart, which it occupied and illuminated permanently. The brain was busy. The light now took its place in his cells, in his nerves, and in his organs. The members were also illuminated.

The boy's eyes, his sense of smell, his hearing, his tongue, his arms, his feet, and his whole body were now one with this light of grace. He turned to the belligerents who had not yet realized the choice of the sphere. They were still in their conflict. As far as the eye could see, it was horror.

The radiant boy opened his arms at last. He raised his hand, indexing the sky. Mercy was granted. Lightning flashed through the fertile clouds. The sky growled. Ropes fell.

Everyone was soaked to the skin. Consciousness slowly returned to the heads. Hearts lit up again. The defilements began to crumble. People began to realize their situations. The arms were dropped one by one. And the hearts calmed themselves progressively. Everyone was wondering why the choice of the little child, but nobody had an answer. Thus, a giant screen appeared in each consciousness, showing the different scenes of their turpitudes and the choice of the child.

They finally understood and reproached themselves shamefully their attitudes. The child disappeared into the mass, although he was spotted and identified by some.

*****

The luminous vortex returned in the opposite direction. All disappeared into the ward of the boy, who was still sitting on a sand dune. This state was accompanied by a great sigh, as if his breathing was restrained. He turned his head slightly toward the four cardinal points and saw only the scenery of his usual landscape. Sand dominated the landscape. He saw a little further away a group of young children his age playing hide-and-seek. A little further, camels picked up the few fruits of thorny fallen to the ground. He got up and stood on the dune, scanning the horizon. No indication of his phantasmagorical world was perceived. He looked from behind and saw the little town built of brick and stone. He reassured himself and joined the small group of children.

The boy had just had an extraordinary experience. He had just been crowned with the supreme jewel, the Pearl of Perfection, but it seemed like one of his dreams. He used to attend events in phantasmagorical worlds, even if he did not understand the expenses of his graces.

He was only five years old, but now the angels never left him, even if he was not aware of their presence. His light spectrum and his magnetism had changed. Nevertheless, it was stamped with the celestial mark, the symbol of the chest, the formula of the supreme name, the symbol that he had drawn so much on the sand without knowing its significance.

The signs were obvious but could only be perceived by those who knew how to see the whispers of the winds, by those who could hear the rustle of the invisible in the sidereal silence.

*****

After this narration, the Sufi shook his head for understanding. Thus, it was up to the host to speak again.

"Do you understand?"

"Yes. I think I understood."

"What did you understand?"

"To be honest, it's a mystery. It is not enough to be a beloved. It will also take perfection to be near the treasure."

"And?"

"It's a child who holds the key. He is also the source of divine mercy."

"And?"

"It is in a desert area, in a small village built of brick."

"I think you got it right. You have to use what is in you to find it. Your guidance is refined."

A few moments later, a tramp with unclean rags and a smile on both ends of his lips came out of one of the alleys and passed in front of them. At their height, he paused and greeted them at length as if he knew the host. He was not slow to respond to this mark of recognition with great fervor.

After the departure of the tramp, the host changed the subject.

"Individuals are classified into four broad groups: those who possess great things and who hope to possess them in the future, those who do not possess them and who do not hope for them in the future, those who do not possess much and hopefully in the future, and finally, those who have great things and do not hope for them in the future."

The Sufi shook his head as an affirmation. However, the host continued, "Those who have great things and hope to own them in the future. They have no worries the next day. Those who do not have big things and who hope for them in the future. They are combative, and they try to move forward because their promise is before them. Those who have much and who do not hope for the future. They curl up on their property and become conservative. And finally, those who do not have much and who do not hope for it in the future. They do not move forward, they do not try to move forward, and they do not let others advance."

After his argument, the Sufi asked him a question.

"And what about this tramp?"

With a peaceful voice, he answered, "It is part of something that has a lot and hopes to own it in the future."

Surprised at his answer, the Sufi tried to rectify the remarks, but the scholar persisted, fixing him in the eyes. Confused and before the persistence of the master, he ended up asking another question of clarification that was soon to find an answer.

"He has faith, which is a great thing. And he hopes to go to heaven, which is another great thing.

The Sufi ended up shaking his head positively for understanding. Thus, the Sufi concluded, "So what is a big thing is not necessarily material but rather virtues."

At these conclusions, the host took the cup of coffee and finished its contents at once. The conversation seemed over. The Sufi lingered to finish his cup and stared at his host, as if trying to find new questions in his head. He came down from his stool, inviting him to look the other way. He took out some coins and handed them to the seller.

Moments later, we could see them through the streets of the shantytown, talking as if they had known each other forever.

At an angle, the native spoke. "This is where my companionship stops."

He waved and left him.

The Sufi tried to unravel the mystery of his host, but he found only a simple man like all the others. He remained frozen on the character until his disappearance at another corner of the street.

# The Voice

Bicycle horns were heard from the living room. The Sufi covered himself with pajamas and went out of the house. A young man on his bike handed him a roll of newspaper. He took it and went back to the house.

In the living room, he removed the rubber band that kept him wrapped and then found a daily newspaper, a magazine, and an advertisement. He flipped through the newspaper briefly and did not seem to find any interesting news. He took the advertisement, watched it for a moment before putting it on the coffee table. He finally took the magazine whose cover page bears in large characters: "THE SAHARA."

He flipped through a page that showed a succession of dunes as far as the eye could see. On another page, a caravan of camels in single file was perched on the peaks of the dunes. He paid attention to it and lost himself in the world of dreams.

A moment later, he came back to him. Another page showed a group of Tuaregs, in a circle, sitting on the floor. Their white and light-blue clothes seemed to abjure with the beige monotony of the sand.

In another page were shown outcrops of an ancient oceanic crust. To say that this desert area was at the bottom of an old disappeared sea would sound bad, but the strata of the sedimentary rock clearly explain some calcified organisms that lived there. The presence of shells is also a witness of an ancient sea presence.

On another page, in a cave, prehistoric drawings showed a savannah, where large game was abundant. Wild animals shared the scenery with hunters, elephants, giraffes, rhinos, and other large mammals. On the same page, a small picture showed the current state of the place: not the shadow of life, everything is sandy.

Another page showed a solitary shrub in a desert area as far as the eye could see. This enigmatic presence in this area that was not raining had been more in ink than the previous pages. In this respect, the Sufi took all his time to read the whole text.

Another passage showed a green oasis amid a monotony of dunes, and next to it was mentioned: "*Ksar, the most remote place in the civilized world.*"

He watched the landscape briefly, then as he changed pages, a voice shook in his mind. *This is the place where the one you are looking for lives.*

He turned his head slightly but saw no one in the living room. He has no doubt heard the voice, but his provenance was a mystery to him. He returned to the page delicately, and the words of the star of perfection came back to him. He stared at the picture immediately and seemed to have seen it in his dreams. Thus, he scanned the houses and alleys in labyrinth. And that was exactly the description of the last star he had met. His certainty of having found the hiding place of what he was looking for was obvious.

Sighs of relief escaped him and tears fell on his cheeks. It was the apotheosis. He wiped them off, then put the magazine on the table without flipping through the remaining pages.

*****

A few days later, the Sufi was in Timbuktu. He went to inquire about the next caravan for Ksar. The response he received seemed to taunt him. "*There is only one caravan every six months.*"

The following days, he made small excursions in the weekly market without forgetting to go around the city. He contemplated the cultural cross-breeding of Bedouins and sub-Saharans.

One day, out of the city and in front of a semidesert and dusty horizon, he turned toward the direction of Ksar by grazing a long rosary. He saw a tree from afar and then walked toward it.

Under the sparse shading, the pearls passed on his fingers. He took a moment to breathe fresh air under a leaden sky.

Moments later, lost in the rhythm of his incantations, he saw himself on a dune, overlooking the Ksar. All his senses seemed refined to their paroxysm. He watched from afar a group of women, in single file, carrying pottery and going toward the lake. His attention was drawn to the last woman on the tail. All the other women were dressed in black-and-white boubous with black scarves, except the last one, who wore a red scarf. Questions about this peculiarity crossed his mind without any answer.

Suddenly, a noise brought him back to his original reality. He saw himself again under the shade next to the tree. A car had just passed behind, raising the dust. He casted his gaze to the horizon and no longer saw Ksar. This vision seemed real because there was movement, but the image on the magazine came back constantly and made him give up his unanswered questions.

A moment later, he returned to the city, waiting for the next caravan. Near the market, a vehicle in excess of speed projected some droplets of muddy water, coming from a small flac, toward the Sufi. The latter landed on his feet indefinitely. Suddenly, a voice trembled in his heart.

*Let me kill him*, the voice said to him.

He froze in his being and was aware that the manifest voice emanated from his heart. And that, this one was different from the one he had heard by his ears.

"No! Leave them," replied the Sufi, watching the vehicle move away.

Smiles escaped him without being surprised at what had happened. Yet this had never happened to him. He stood there, contemplating the environment without any feelings. Moments later, he returned to his inn.

# The Big Meeting

While waiting for the next caravan to Ksar, the Sufi spent most of his time investigating the Ksar, its people, its customs, and its particularity. Gradually, he conformed to the culture of Ksar, the desert, even going so far as to adopt their fashion dress.

One day, as usual, he made small excursions in the weekly market without forgetting to go around the city. A special sensation of meeting someone crossed his mind. He remained a moment to scrutinize the different paths of the market leading to him but did not see any knowledge. He remembered the antique dealer with whom he had shared his fortune. Finding no one, he continued on his way.

The next day, at the same place, the event occurred. He crossed the antiquary with great astonishment. No one was waiting for the other in this remote area of the world, and especially if it was a place on another continent.

After fraternal and warm embraces, he ended up articulating.

"What are you doing here?" asked the Sufi.

"That's the same question I wanted to ask you. Me, I always dreamed of visiting Timbuktu, but I never had enough money for this trip. So when you had given me this fortune, I could not do without this dream of coming to inquire about the 333 saints buried in the city and their wise teachings. I told myself that if they were called saints, it was inevitably that they had contributed much to the evolution of humanity with wisdom. And you?"

"I want to go to Ksar to find answers to my quest."

"It is true that we are all in search of something, and that we will not be appeased until we see it come true. It's our self, our den signs inscribed on the big table of destinies."

"And what is amazing, yesterday in the same place, I had the impression to meet you here, even when nothing presaged."

Like a scholar, the septuagenarian expressed himself, "There is no chance. We are all interconnected to reality. It is enough simply to listen to hear, to look to see, and to try to realize what one is pre-disposed in the labyrinth of infinite choices.

Thus, the words of the onirocritic returned to him: *"One has beautiful to dream .... there is only the real one."*

They remained talking for long moments before leaving each other.

\*\*\*\*\*

In the fourth month of waiting, a caravan had finally been formed. He bought the transport services of ten camels, which he loaded with gifts for the inhabitants of the oasis.

After several weeks of traveling under a leaden sky during the day and a cold coldness at night, they finally saw the palm groves of the oasis at a distance. A sigh of relief was shown on the attitudes of travelers.

Little by little, some dunes overlooking the oasis filled with children. The caravan was greeted by clamor, accompanied by ancestral songs. Wreaths of palm were brandished as a sign of victory. Their men were back, and they had again conquered the immensity of the desert and its whims. The isolation of the area means that these moments were always synonymous with collective celebration.

In the main square of Ksar, the person in charge of the oasis welcomed them. In the desert custom, this is the first person to be informed of the convoy and its load. The leader of the caravan informed him of the existence of a visitor. He introduced him to the Sufi. At this warm meeting, the head of the oasis invited him to be his guest in his home, which is a great honor in the Bedouin custom.

Most people in the oasis had never seen another person from a different culture. Everyone wanted to meet the newcomer who had different racial characteristics of the natives. A crowd of curious crowded into the house of the chief. Without delay, the chief ordered the preparation of the tea. Around this atmosphere, questions and answers about other horizons ensued. It was the only way for the inhabitants of the oasis to change their daily lives.

The Sufi distributed the gifts. All the children were invited to pick up theirs. After the meeting of the latter, the Sufi saw no sign showing him the one he was looking for. At the end of the cast, he turned slightly to the chef and asked if that was all. He checked with the count and confirmed the exact number of children.

The Sufi, sure of the child's absence, insisted on the chief. The latter checked and reconfirmed his answer.

"All the children present in the oasis are there," said the chief.

A moment later, as crossed by another consciousness, the leader turned slightly to the Sufi, rectifying his words, "I was wrong. There is another child, Makham, but he is absent from the oasis."

Jumping in excitement, the Sufi soon asked him where he was.

"He accompanied his father to the salt mines. It is our custom to introduce the child to the father's work in their fifth year," said the chief.

The chef found the faces in the small crowd of his house but did not see what he was looking for. He waved a hand, and then a teenager came over and whispered. He whispered a few words before turning to Sufi.

"I sent him to call the mother. She will be able to keep his gift until his return."

A moment later, a young lady arrived. Eyes wide-open, the Sufi did not look away from her, while it is forbidden to watch married women at length. His eyes aroused a few whispers in the crowd.

Indeed, it was the same woman he had seen in his vision at the door of Timbuktu. The woman was wearing the same clothes, with a red scarf as in his vision when he had never seen her. He now knew that Makham was the holder of the key to the heavenly chest.

"Where is he?" asked the Sufi.

His eagerness was so great that he transgressed the laws of the community again by addressing the woman directly. She hesitated to answer him. Thus, he reiterated his question without any response from the woman. He ended up understanding the woman's dubious attitude.

To rectify his mistake, he finally turned to the chief.

"How am I going to meet him?" asked the Sufi.

"You do not need. Just give it to his mother. She will keep it until his return," replied the chief.

"I would like to give it to him myself as I did for the other children here."

Faced with the incomprehension of the chief, the Sufi explained, "It will allow me to honor him as much as I did for others."

This mark of wisdom and gratitude to his community touched the heart of the leader. His eyes sparkled with joy.

"Where he is, is three days walk. It is far," clarified the chief.

"Let me pay for the services of a guide to take me there," insisted the Sufi.

Faced with this obstinacy, the chief hesitated a moment, and then granted him his request.

The next day, the Sufi was accompanied by three other riders on dromedary.

Three days later, at the zenith, they arrived at the salt mine. One of the horsemen addressed the father of Makham, explaining to them their arrival on the authorization of the head of their community. He greeted him warmly.

Goblets of slightly fermented camel milk were served to newcomers.

"You're really lucky because we were getting ready to leave in the afternoon. You see, the camels are already loaded. While we'll be back here only after several months," Makham's father announced.

The Sufi took out the gift he had reserved for Makham, who did not hesitate to pick him up before he was handed it to him.

After receiving his present, Makham scrutinized him for a moment, and then addressed the Sufi as a scholar.

"What is the hidden face?" Makham asked him.

"Of course, only God knows what is veiled by his mystery. He is the savant, the mighty," replied the Sufi.

He summed up his answer about the four stars he had met.

Makham sketched a small smile before continuing, "You have been well-guided. The key to your worries is very far from here. It is in the continent from which you come. It is an old and twisted horn on which is engraved its own key. Just stroke it three times from left to right before pronouncing the formula as many times. You will have your instrument to blow to repel this destiny."

At once, the Sufi is lost in the world of dreams. His old horn, which he had bought from the antiquary, came back to him, but he did not remember any engraving.

Certainly, his horn that he had exposed in his living room was old and twisted, but old horns and twisted could be found in all the countries of his adopted continent.

*"Most say that the horns cannot be bought, just go to the slaughter-house to find for free galore,"* the antiquary had told him.

Finding the horn with the right formula would be as dangerous as his quest for the key keeper of the heavenly chest because the continent was huge and with dozens of countries.

"And how am I going to find the horn?" asked the Sufi.

"You searched for me while I was hidden, and you found me."

"There, I was well-guided. And I only followed the signs."

"You dreamed, and then you made wishes. You worked through the journey, which allowed you to be guided and to have some knowledge of certain virtues that facilitated your access to perfection. Having used his essence, you found me. From now on, you can modify this unfortunate destiny in order to retreat this last day of the world until the end of time. Just listen to you."

He lost himself in the world of the past and immediately remembered the third star that traumatized passersby with his words that some might call heresy. When he had offered him the ring, it had no value in his eyes when it was the ring of Solomon, an inestimable relic. He remembered throwing it in a garbage bin. And for several days, he did not even care about his future. He remembered that he was not the only one to underestimate the ring since during his last farewell ballad, an individual who had picked up the ring near the trash had repeated the same gestures as him by projecting the jewel after having scrutinized it.

*"Only God knows. He is the source of truth,"* the third star of wisdom had told him.

He returned to his original reality and looked admirably at the child.

The last words of Makham reassured him because it came from the one who was the object of his quest, with all its vicissitudes. He did not get what he expected, but the hope of finding the right horn appeased him.

# The Unveiling

A few weeks later, he was back in his adoptive country. In his living room, for a brief moment, his eyes passed on his old horn exposed on the coffee table of the living room. A surprising attitude crossed him. He came back on the horn and stared at it for a moment before concluding that he did not see any formula.

For more than two hours, his mind was searching for the place where the salvating horn should be. From country to country, from region to region, no convincing idea reached him. He imagined the model of the horn. With his mind, he defiled on different types of animal horns to the most exotic. This brief diagnosis did not miss wildebeest, impala, hartebeest, cobs, damalisques, nilgauts, oryx, scimitar, saiga, or springbok.

A moment later, in front of his tiredness, he went to take the horn, then looked at it again but saw no inscription. His heart made him try to follow Makham's instructions anyway. He caressed the left horn right then briefly appeared a few letters in light before disappearing. It was a great surprise on his part. He tried again for a second time.

More letters of light appeared. The inscription remained longer visible before disappearing again.

It was the apotheosis. He knew more than ever that he had found what he was looking for after so many years of vicissitudes. His eyes dripped. Despite the repeated wiping, his tears continued to flow. For several months, he had traveled to the most remote areas of the civilized world in his quest as he was facing what he was looking for.

The antiquary had kept the horn for forty years, without finding a person to sell it for, while he kept it only for the Sufi. His benevolence had borne fruit since the Sufi had paid him half of his fortune, which made him a very rich man who could even realize his childhood dreams.

The memories of his journeys since the beginning of his quest ran through his mind. The image of onirocriticism came back to him, his trip to the mausoleum of the supreme relief with his dream of guidance, his meeting with the stevedore, the first star of wisdom with the dark man who wanted to transfer his evil, his initiatory master with its methodology, the second star and the third star with its old-fashioned ring, which is the one of Solomon and which was invaluable, the antique dealer who possessed great wisdom and who had dreamed since childhood only to go to visit Timbuktu, the fourth star with his sartorial simplicity, and finally the child, the concealed one.

He ended his tears and said to himself, "Really, what is veiled by the mystery of the divine transcends the eyes of ordinary mortals."

He stroked the horn for a third time. Thus, the complete formula in bright light appeared permanently. He turned the horn to read the formula that followed the spiral shape of the horn.

It was written: *"In the name of the first, the last, the visible and the hidden."*

Still following Makham's instructions, he pronounced the formula three times. Immediately, the horn revived. She unfolded. She turned into a gold horn. She twinkled with several rays.

At the end of his agitation, the Sufi never stopped saying, "The trumpet of the archangel Israfil!"

He made the vow that tapped him from the beginning of his quest *"peace return to earth,"* then blew into the trumpet.

Ropes of angels came out of the other end of the musical instrument. They filled the living room before invading the world.

In this respect, the trumpet dissipated in multitudes seeds of light before disappearing.

*****

At the same time, the staffs of the two blocks were camped in their respective secret bunkers in order to fight back against any nuclear attack. The wait was long. The silence was sidereal.

With a start, the president of the republic of the spy bloc tried to pick up the phone.

"I'll call them," the president decided.

He was instantly dissuaded by some generals, who thought it would be a sign of weakness. After a little hesitation, the president eventually landed the aircraft, despite the insistence of his generals.

At the other end of the line, another phone on the command table, surrounded by the other block's chairman's team, rang. Nobody will react. The phone reiterated his call a second time, then a third time, without being dropped. On his fourth ring, the president's heart seemed to be appeased by the insistence of his counterpart. He ended up dropping.

"Hello, Igor," greeted the appellant president.

The other president was slow to respond to this invitation of reverence. Suddenly, a rush of anger can be seen on the features of his face. However, the appellant continued, "I'm really sorry about what had happened. We are ready to negotiate and fix our mistakes. We compensate you for all the damage. At least, this is due to humanity after so many centuries of construction. A war would only mean annihilation and you know it. Your decision is peremptory for the salvation of humanity."

At these apologetic remarks, President Igor seemed to be appeased. He gave a little sigh before answering, "You know it was a declaration of war. We held ourselves back."

"We are aware of this, and we regret what had happened."

A brief moment of silence was made, and he spoke again.

"We will give you the date and place of the meeting," simplified President Igor.

"Thanks anyway for this kindness. Thank you, my friend. We are grateful to you."

*****

A few weeks later, a summit gathering of the different belligerents was organized. In this respect, several negotiations were conducted. And this was the beginning of a long process of negotiations for the effective control of the proliferation of weapons of mass destruction.

Precarious peace returned. The world opened more. Communication broadens on humanitarian concerns. The exchanges developed. The consciousness came back. And finally, the last day of the world was postponed until the end of time.

To be continued.

# About the Author

Dr. El Hadji Seydou Mbaye was born in 1978 in Kaolack, a region of Senegal. During 2008 to 2013, he persued his PhD in biology and human pathologies, with the collaboration of the International Agency for Research on Cancer (IARC) / WHO, Lyon (France). In 2006 to 2007, master of life and health, specialty biology of microorganisms, virology in Louis Pasteur University of Strasbourg (France). In 2005 to 2006, master of life and health, option of immuno-physiopathology in Louis Pasteur University of Strasbourg (France). In 2004 to 2005, B.Sc of biochemistry in Louis Pasteur University of Strasbourg (France). In 2002 to 2004, general degree in sciences and technologies in University of METZ (France).

He was certified by the Federation International of Gynecology Obstetrics (FIGO), the Accreditation Council of Oncology in Europe (ACOE, www.acoe.be), and the Institute Catalan of Oncology (ICO) for cervical cancer prevention (grade 10/10) in support of continuing medical education for physicians. These credits are also recognized as Physician's Recognition Award (AMA PRA Category 1 credits) by the American Medical Association. He was awarded as prestigious editor, as Best Reviewer 2019, as International Outstanding Scientist Awards 2020, as International Best Researcher Awards 2021, as International Excellence Service Award 2022, as International Best Innovation Award 2022, and as Certificate of Excellence in Reviewing. He was certified by the United Nations for Basic Notion of Security on the Ground-Protection, health and behavior, by the International Agency for Research on Cancer (IARC)/World Health Organization, Lyon (France) for safety certificate, and by Save the Children for Personal Safety and Security. He has published one book with a style of philosophical story. Author of the world program against cancer in low- and middle-income countries; he is the lead author (first listed) of more than ninety peer-reviewed research articles published in reputed journals. He was appointed as editor-in-chief of four scientific journals. He was review board member of thirteen scientific journals and editorial board member of 157 scientific peer-reviewed journals. He was associate membership of the World Society for Virology (WSV), member of Allied Academies, member of Helics Group, member of World's Leading Virologist Group (Facing to COVID-19), member of U.S. National Academies of Sciences, Engineering, and Medicine (NASEM): Societal Experts Action Network (SEAN), and also member of BCNet International Working Group, International Agency for Research on Cancer (IARC)/World Health Organization (WHO).

Dr. Mbaye has participated in the first two "Nobel Prize Summit," and also he was candidate in the first two "World Society for Virology" elections. Dr. Mbaye has formed, for free, more than 250 health care professionals for the techniques of cervical cancer screening in Senegal. He has screened, for free, more than two thousand women in Senegal. He has appeared on local media: 2S TV, Mbour TV, Leeral.net, 7TV, and Sen TV.

Printed in the USA
CPSIA information can be obtained
at www.ICGtesting.com
CBHW031252230624
10522CB00007B/168